Exciting

Diana looked up at Jeremy, suddenly remembering that he was the boy Sasha had said might be in one of her classes. The idea made her heartbeat quicken. He was cute and friendly and if they were both strangers to the school, it would give them something in common. She was suddenly acutely conscious of Jeremy Stone's intense gaze.

"I'd like to photograph you, Diana," he said, coming closer. "You have terrific bone structure, and with those dark eyes, and your blonde hair, you could be a model."

Diana smiled at the earnestness of his expression, captivated by the sparkle in his eyes, and the honesty in his gaze. "I'll think about it, Jeremy," she promised, hoping that he wouldn't change his mind after school opened. There was something very exciting about Jeremy Stone — something that made Diana want to know him better.

Books from Scholastic
in the **Couples** series:

Couples Special Edition
Summer Heat!

COUPLES

PICTURE PERFECT

by M.E. Cooper

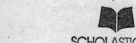

SCHOLASTIC INC.
New York Toronto London Auckland Sydney

ISBN 0-590-40237-4

12 11 10 9 8 7 6 5 4 3 2 1   8   6 7 8 9/8 0 1/9

Printed in the U.S.A.   06

PICTURE PERFECT

Chapter

1

Gloria Macmillan looked up as a car pulled into the driveway across the street. Ever since the Greenes had sold their house, she'd lived in dread that someone truly awful would move in. Now she was finally going to get a look at the new residents.

Braced for the worst — a half-dozen screaming toddlers — she almost clapped with delight when an extremely handsome guy emerged from the station wagon. Tall, brawny, with a deep tan and dark hair, he appeared to be about seventeen or eighteen, and he was gorgeous.

"Talk about improving the neighborhood," she murmured to herself. Her enthusiasm waned a little as a very pretty girl followed him out of the car. She looked younger, but she was tall, blonde, and willowy.

"Why don't you go over and introduce yourself, Gloria?" her mother suggested, coming out on the porch to join her.

"I don't know," Gloria began, half wanting to, if only to be the first to meet that handsome guy. It sounded like the right thing to do, but what if they didn't feel like meeting anyone yet? After all, they'd just pulled in to the driveway. "Maybe they already know people in Rose Hill," she said.

"From what I've heard, their father is a newly-elected congressman and he and his wife just bought the house and brought the children here from Montana."

"Montana?" Gloria arched a dark eyebrow. "Come to think of it, he does look something like a cowboy."

"So be a good neighbor and introduce yourself. You could offer to show them around Rose Hill," her mother advised. "Give them a chance to meet some of your friends before school starts Monday."

"I'll do it," Gloria decided, already picturing the impact she would have if she walked into the sub shop in the company of the boy who'd just gotten out of the station wagon. No one would be able to ignore her if she was on his arm.

It had been a pretty awful summer, thanks to the way Laurie Bennington had accused her of disrupting the student government elections at Kennedy High last spring. Farley Templar, Gloria's boyfriend at the time, had lost the election and they'd broken up not too long afterward. There'd been no one to take his place since then, and she'd spent most of the summer alone.

2

Gloria sighed, forcing the memories away. A new school year was starting, and this year she was going to make sure she was part of the crowd that made things happen at Kennedy. She just had to be. She'd had a taste of the fun they had when she'd served as Laurie's campaign manager for the election. Ever since then she'd been trying to fit in, but nothing had worked yet. All she needed was one more chance, and this just might be it.

She hurried inside to put on fresh lip gloss and to make sure that the light breeze hadn't destroyed her carefully arranged chestnut hair. Then, squaring her shoulders, she adjusted her bright orange-colored tank top and made sure there were no grass stains on her white shorts.

The front door of the house stood open and Gloria hesitated at the curb, trying to see inside. As the girl came out, Gloria put on her best smile and hurried across the street. "Hi," she called. I'm Gloria Macmillan, and I think we're going to be neighbors."

"Oh, hi." The girl looked startled and shy, then she smiled. "I'm Diana Einerson. Do you live around here?"

Gloria pointed toward the white house she'd just left. "Welcome to Rose Hill," she said, feeling like a one-woman Welcome Wagon and hating it. Trust her mother to have a dumb idea like this. You didn't just walk up to people and introduce yourself; she should have just waited until school started Monday.

"Hello there." A soft deep voice interrupted her thoughts. When Gloria turned around, she could

3

see that the boy was even better-looking close up than he was from across the street. His eyes were a dark brown, and his smile was slow and lazy. "Who might you be?" he asked.

Diana made the introductions, but Gloria heard very little beyond his name — Bart Einerson. It fit him perfectly. She forced her brain into operation and managed to ask a few polite questions about their arrival and where they'd come from. Diana didn't talk much, but from Bart Gloria quickly learned that Diana was to be a junior like Gloria, and Bart was a senior.

Gloria flashed Bart a big smile. "If you two would like, I could take you over to the sub shop later this afternoon," she began. "It's a pretty popular place and I could introduce you to whoever is around."

"That sounds terrific," Bart said, looking deep into her eyes and making her heart skip a beat. "I'm sure Mom will let us take the car as soon as we get it unloaded."

"I'll go home and change then," Gloria murmured. "How soon do you want to go?"

"About an hour?" Bart suggested.

"I'll be back," Gloria promised, including Diana in her smile. It would be nice to have a friend in her own class at school. Farley had taken so much of her time last year that she'd lost touch with her friends. Diana seemed shy, but with a brother like Bart, she could have as many friends as she wanted. Gloria hurried back across the street, thinking about what she could put on that would be sure to attract Bart's attention.

"Well," Bart said as soon as he and Diana were

alone, "she was nice to come over, don't you think?"

"I can't imagine why a pretty girl would come over to meet us," Diana teased. She was used to seeing girls flock around her big brother; they'd been after him since he entered junior high school back in Helena. "Think you'll ask her out?"

Bart opened the back of the station wagon and lifted several suitcases out, then shrugged. "I think I'll wait and see what the rest of the girls are like."

Diana shook her head. If Bart hadn't been her brother, she would have considered him a wolf. As it was, she knew that his easy charm covered many of the same doubts and fears she felt about moving here. It was easier for him, though, because he wasn't as shy as she was. But she knew he wasn't happy about spending his senior year in a new school instead of graduating with all his friends.

"So what about you, Diana?" Bart asked. "Did you like her?"

Diana shrugged, thinking longingly of Sally and Barbara, the close friends she'd left behind. Right now she couldn't imagine being able to confide in someone as aggressive and sophisticated as Gloria Macmillan, but that was just her first impression. The friends she had known were the kind of people who grew up on the next ranch and experienced all the same crises — like being stranded in a blizzard or spending all night taking care of a sick horse. This new life was certainly going to take some getting used to.

"What are you two doing out there?" their

5

mother called from the doorway. "I thought you were unloading the car."

"We just met one of the neighbors," Bart replied, picking up the two biggest suitcases. "She offered to show us around this afternoon — if you don't need the car."

"You're going out already?" Rose Einerson said, with a hint of disappointment.

"We don't have to, Mom," Diana said quickly. "It's just that it would be nice to see Rose Hill, maybe meet some people before school starts Monday."

"There are a lot of things to check out in a new town, Mom," Bart added, as he disappeared through the door.

Diana picked up the two small suitcases and followed him. "I can stay home," she offered. "I have a feeling Gloria was really only interested in taking Bart around."

"Nonsense, you're both going. Your father won't be home before seven, so there's no reason for you to stay here."

Diana noticed the resentment in her mother's voice as she climbed the stairs to her room to look for something to wear.

"This is it," Gloria announced as they pulled into the parking area. "I know it's not fancy, but the best crowd hangs out here, so. . . ."

"So that's who we want to meet," Bart finished for her.

"It does look interesting," Diana said, wondering if she had dressed appropriately. Gloria had changed into a cotton skirt and blouse that made

6

the most of her curvy figure. Diana felt under-dressed in faded jeans and an oversized yellow cotton-knit sweater.

It was obvious the sub shop was a Kennedy High hangout, with school pennants draped from every rafter. Picnic tables and benches were scattered about the room, and an ancient juke box spilled a steady beat into the air. Diana dubiously eyed the wooden Indian and stuffed polar bear standing guard over the place, as she followed Bart and Gloria across the room.

Gloria walked straight up to a table where four people were sitting. "Hi, everybody," she said. "These are my new neighbors, Diana and Bart. They've just moved to Rose Hill from Montana, and will be starting school at Kennedy on Monday."

The two girls and two boys looked up and smiled politely, but Diana didn't miss the coolness in the way they greeted Gloria. They didn't seem to welcome her like an old friend, but Gloria introduced them all as if she knew them well.

The shorter girl with the long curly red hair and bright green eyes was Phoebe Hall. The brunette with the dreamy dark eyes was Sasha Jenkins, the editor of the high school paper. Peter Lacey was handsome, with wavy brown hair and green eyes, but there was so much charm in his greeting, Diana had a feeling he was used to girls' crushes. The other boy's welcoming grin made her feel instantly comfortable.

"Welcome to our place, Diana, Bart," Woody Webster said, in a gracious, exaggerated voice.

"It ain't much, but it's our home away from home." He stood up and made a sweeping bow. "Our bench is your bench."

"Sit down," Phoebe urged, sliding down the bench on her side of the table as they all giggled at Woody's antics. Bart slid in beside her with a pleased grin. Diana started to follow her brother, but Gloria was too quick for her and took the final space on the bench next to Bart.

For a moment Diana was frozen in embarrassment. She quickly recovered and made up her mind not to let Gloria get to her. Woody smiled at her and patted the bench on his side of the table. "Come and sit down and tell me all about life in the wilds of Montana," he invited.

Diana blushed shyly as she slipped in beside Woody. She sat back and relaxed as Bart began to answer a barrage of questions.

Within minutes he had not only Phoebe, Sasha, and Gloria hanging on his every word, but Peter and Woody, too. They all loved his stories about life on the Lazy E — their ranch outside Helena, Montana. In no time at all Bart seemed like one of the group. Diana still felt shy and awkward and even though everyone was being friendly, she couldn't help wishing she were more outgoing like Bart.

When his monologue ended, everyone started talking at once and Diana found herself chatting with Sasha and Woody about Kennedy High. She was starting to relax as she realized they were all trying to make her feel comfortable and accepted. She couldn't help wondering about Gloria, though. From the way she spoke, Diana got the

8

feeling she didn't really spend much time with these people. Diana glanced over at her and saw her engaged in a conversation with Phoebe.

"Are you anxious for school to start, Phoebe?" Gloria asked, smiling hopefully at the redhead. "I mean, now that you're going to be a senior?"

"In some ways, I am," Phoebe said. "After all, senior year is supposed to be the most exciting and wonderful and. . . ." Her words trailed off as another couple came through the door.

"Here come Henry and Janie," she said, waving them over. Phoebe introduced Bart and Diana to Henry Braverman and Janie Barstow.

"So how is your design business going, Henry?" Gloria asked.

"Almost too well," the tall, sandy-haired Henry answered. "I haven't had much time for anything else this summer."

Janie smiled, her delicate features lighting up as she looked at Henry. "He's done the most wonderful designs," she said softly. "I just wish we could have another fashion show at school to display them."

"School hasn't even started yet," Woody protested, "but once it does, maybe we can come up with something."

"Trust you to volunteer," Phoebe teased. She explained to Diana and Bart, "Woody is very good at organizing and directing shows and things. He likes to see the rest of us working."

"Someone has to organize all of you," he said in a mournful tone that made them all laugh. "If it weren't for me, you'd just study and have fun. That's *not* what school is about."

"I'd love to see your new designs, Henry," Gloria interrupted. "In fact, maybe you could make a dress for me the way you did for Phoebe and Sasha and Janie last year."

"I'll bet you're his inspiration, aren't you, Janie?" Bart asked, sending his sexiest grin across the table to her.

"She's my favorite model, that's for sure," Henry agreed, putting his arm around Janie. Bart paid no attention to him. His gaze was locked with Janie's.

"I just had a great idea," Sasha said, changing the subject. "I think I'll do an interview series for *The Red and the Gold* — that's our school paper — to introduce the new transfer students to the rest of the student body."

"Starting with Bart and Diana Einerson, of course," Phoebe said.

"Well, they are the first new students I've met," Sasha reminded her. "Except for Jeremy Stone." She smiled at Diana. "He's Monica Ford's cousin from London. His father is a diplomat assigned to the embassy in Washington and Jeremy will be a junior, too. Maybe you'll have some classes with him. He's real nice."

"He'll probably talk your ears off asking about the West and cowboys and everything," Woody said. "He's positively demented on the subject of anything American."

Diana smiled. "Do you know if there's any place around here to rent horses?" she asked.

Woody considered for a moment, then said, "I think Danberry Stable has a few horses to rent out. You'll have to ask John Marquette about that. His sister and brother-in-law own the place."

"Why don't you just call the stable and ask instead," Sasha suggested. "You don't want to talk to John Marquette, Diana."

"Haven't you heard about the new, improved Marquette, Sasha?" Woody asked. "The guys on the football team say he's really changed a lot over the summer."

"Unless he had a total personality transplant, it won't be enough," Sasha said.

"Well, here's your chance to see who's right," Peter said. "Look who's coming."

Diana looked up and caught her breath as a tall, athletic-looking guy entered. He wore faded Levis and a knit shirt that showed off an impressive number of muscles. His smile was confident as he crossed to the table.

"Board of Directors meeting?" he inquired, when his eyes met Diana's and the arrogance vanished from his expression. "Well, hello there. Who are you?" he asked.

Woody introduced Bart and Diana, then moved aside grudgingly to make room for John. "We were just talking about you," he said.

"Don't believe a thing they told you, Diana," John said, his eyes never leaving her face. "They're just jealous." His tone was meant to be bantering, but she sensed some genuine feeling beneath the words.

"Actually, I suggested that you might be the one to help the Einersons find a riding stable," Woody said, no longer teasing. "Your sister and her husband run Danberry Stable, don't they?"

"You like to ride?" John looked pleased. "Hey,

11

that's great. I spent part of the summer at this fitness camp and they had a fantastic riding program. I loved it."

"I grew up on a ranch in Montana," Diana explained, conscious of all the eyes upon her. "We just moved here and I thought . . . well, I sort of miss my horses."

"Why don't we go riding tomorrow?" John suggested. "I'm sure my sister Irene has some decent horses." His lingering gaze was flattering, but she was relieved when he seemed to remember that Bart was at the table, too. "You can come, too, Bart," he said, his invitation half-hearted now.

Bart's eyes met Diana's and he grinned slyly. "Thanks, but I think I have other plans for tomorrow afternoon." His gaze went from Phoebe to Sasha to Gloria, his lazy grin resting on each of them.

"Bart's a football player, John," Woody said.

"Really?" John's gaze appraised Diana's brother.

"Our team won every game for two years in a row," Bart answered proudly. "My freshman year I wasn't on the team."

"You just might be what we need to clean up this year," John said. "I'll be sure and introduce you to the right people." His tone made it clear that he didn't consider Peter, Woody, or Henry in that category. He turned back to Diana with a gentle smile. "About one o'clock tomorrow afternoon?" he asked. "You'll have to give me your address."

Diana hesitated. She really wanted to go riding, but she didn't even know this guy.

"Please don't say no," he continued. "I know you'll like my sister and her horses."

The temptation was too great to refuse. John Marquette reminded her of Freddy Welch, Bart's one-time best friend and the first boy she'd ever dated. "I'd love to go," she said. "And thank you for asking me."

"Oh, it's my pleasure, little lady," he said, sounding a lot like a character from an old Western movie. "Now, if you'll give me your address, I've got to bolt. I'm supposed to stop in at Superjock — the biggest sporting goods store in D.C. My cousin owns it and I work there part-time."

Diana wrote her address on a napkin, using a pen borrowed from Sasha. Her fingers were trembling and she watched John Marquette leave with a mixture of relief and disappointment. Maybe it wouldn't be so bad here after all.

Chapter 2

"Do you believe that?" Sasha gasped. "Was that really John Marquette? I mean, it sort of looked like him, but. . . . What in the world happened to him this summer?"

"Fitness camp had a real effect on him," Woody replied. "Ted's seen him every day at football practice and says he came back a changed man."

"Well, he certainly looks different," Phoebe said. "He used to be pretty beefy. He sure has lost weight."

"He acted like a human being, too," Sasha commented.

"Is there something wrong with the guy?" Bart asked. "I mean, he did just ask my sister out, so if there's something I should know. . . ."

Before Diana could protest over Bart's protective attitude, Gloria interrupted. "I think John Marquette just wants to be accepted like everybody else. He's always been very nice to me, and I'm sure he'll treat Diana just fine. He seemed to like her a lot."

"I've never seen Marquette act so normal around a girl before," Woody observed with a grin. "Diana, I think you may have been responsible for one of the great miracles of our time."

Diana felt the heat in her cheeks again, but she managed to smile as everyone else laughed at Woody's words. She was about to say something when the group's attention was claimed once again by another new face at the door.

"Hiya, Jeremy," Peter called. "Come on over. We have some new people for you to meet."

Diana looked up, grateful for the change of subject. Her date with John had seemed like such a good idea at first, but she was beginning to have doubts. Nobody at the table seemed to be too crazy about him. She turned her attention to the good-looking boy approaching.

Jeremy came toward the table, his thick brown hair bouncing a little with his quick movements. He wasn't as tall or as muscular as John Marquette, but his stride radiated energy and when he smiled, his blue-gray eyes flashed with excitement. "What's going on?" he asked with a marked English accent.

"Gloria just brought her new neighbors over," Phoebe explained, then introduced Bart and Diana. "Jeremy is Monica Ford's cousin," she went on. "Monica and Peter work together at WKND, the school radio station. Peter is our resident DJ, in case you hadn't noted those resonant tones."

Peter stood up to take a bow. "And Jeremy is a secret agent sent over from England to find out what Americans are really like. You two should be warned to watch out at all times. He has more cameras than *People* magazine and he's always taking photographs of everything in sight."

"Peter is just camera shy," Woody teased. "I, on the other hand, see true genius in this import and am looking forward to his video tapes of all the school productions this year. Save our best efforts for posterity and all that."

"You mean be sure that our mistakes can haunt us forever," Phoebe corrected. "I shudder to think what those tapes will look like to us in five years."

"Blackmail material," Jeremy supplied, chuckling evilly. "The things I've seen through my viewfinder. . . ."

The laughter was easy and Diana found herself giggling along with the others. This really was a fun crowd and she was no longer surprised to find she was having a good time. They weren't at all stiff and formal the way she'd feared they might be and they really seemed interested in her as well as in Bart.

Diana looked up at Jeremy, suddenly remembering that he was the boy Sasha had said might be in some of her classes. The idea made her heartbeat quicken. He was cute and friendly and if they were both strangers to the school, it would give them something in common. She rather hoped that he'd sit down on the bench in the spot John Marquette had recently vacated.

Woody seemed to read her mind. "Why don't

you sit down, Jeremy," he said. "I'd love to know what you've seen through your viewfinder."

"I can't," Jeremy said, looking out the front windows toward the street and parking area. "I'm just waiting for my mother to pick me up. She's somewhere in the area looking at an empty building that might do for a dance school."

Phoebe sighed. "I suppose it is time to be heading home. I promised to help with dinner."

"We probably should be getting home, too, Bart," Diana said. "We haven't even begun to unpack yet." She started to get up, but before she could, Janie reached out and touched her arm.

"It's really been nice to meet you, Diana," she said softly. "I hope we'll have a chance to get better acquainted." Her smile was sweet and genuine, and Diana felt an immediate liking for her. She sensed that Janie might understand her shyness.

"I'd like that, too, Janie," she told her.

"Be careful tomorrow," Janie said. "With John Marquette, I mean. He'd have to have changed an awful lot to be trustworthy."

Diana stiffened at the words, wondering what John Marquette could possibly have done to provoke such a warning. "I . . . uh, thanks, I will," she murmured. "See you," she added to the whole table as Bart and Gloria got up to leave, too.

There was a chorus of casual invitations from the remaining members of the group as Diana got to her feet. She was suddenly acutely conscious of Jeremy Stone's intense gaze and nearly stubbed her toes on the protruding bench at the next table.

17

"I'd like to photograph you, Diana," he said, coming closer. "You have terrific bone structure, and with those dark eyes and your blonde hair, you could be a model."

Diana felt red climbing up her tanned cheeks and she became conscious of the tendrils of hair escaping from her hastily-tied ponytail and the way her sweater kept slipping off one shoulder. What a line, she thought to herself, but she couldn't explain the tingling sensation she felt when her eyes met his.

"Trust the new girl to get all the attention," Gloria said with a petulant smile that didn't reach her hazel eyes.

"You're a new girl, Gloria, as far as I'm concerned," Bart said, putting a light hand on her shoulder. "And I'd be happy to take your picture any time."

"You are sweet, Bart," Gloria cooed up at him, but Diana saw that she was looking over her shoulder at Jeremy Stone as they headed for the door. She shook her head, unable to sort out the complicated relationships within the group.

"I'm serious, Diana," Jeremy said, following her to the door. "I would like to take pictures of you. I think you'd be surprised by what the camera will show."

"Thanks, Jeremy, but. . . ."

"Don't say no," he protested. "I'm really not as awful as Peter says. I won't take your photograph if you don't want me to."

Diana smiled at the earnestness of his expression, captivated by the sparkle in his eyes and the honesty in his gaze. "I'll think about it, Jeremy," she promised, hoping that he wouldn't change his mind after school opened. There was something very exciting about Jeremy Stone — something that made Diana want to know him better.

"Now that was fun," Bart said as they drove out of the parking lot. "I think I'm going to like it here."

"I certainly hope so," Gloria said, batting her eyelashes at him. "And it looks like you're going to fit right in, too. You made a real hit with the group."

"It was very nice of you to introduce us to your friends," Diana murmured politely, aware that Gloria was mostly interested in Bart, not her.

"You made quite a hit, too," Gloria said, surprising her. "A date with John Marquette already and now that cute Jeremy wanting to photograph you — I could be jealous." Her strained laughter was meant to make the words a joke, but Diana had a strange feeling that they were close to the truth.

"Janie didn't seem to like John much," Diana said, remembering the quiet girl's words of warning. "And neither does Sasha. Do you know why?"

"He made a pass at Sasha, I think," Gloria replied. "And he's always teasing Janie. Don't worry about it, just have fun tomorrow. John is a pretty important person at Kennedy High. He's a star athlete and real popular with a lot of people."

"I just hope he really likes to ride," Diana said, thinking that she'd probably feel more secure about everything once she was on a horse. Life had a way of looking more manageable to her when she was riding.

She was glad to get back to the house even though it wasn't really home to her yet.

"So what do you think of everyone, Sis?" Bart asked after Gloria headed home.

"Well, they all seem really nice," Diana ventured. "What about you? What are you going to be doing tomorrow afternoon that's more fun than riding with John and me?"

Bart grinned. "Well, to start with, I've got an appointment to meet Sasha at the sub shop to get started on our interview. She says she wants to print mine first, then Jeremy's and then yours. I'd kind of like to get to know her better."

"She is pretty," Diana conceded, "but didn't I hear that she has a boyfriend? And what about Gloria?"

"What about her?" Bart looked surprised.

"Well, I thought you'd probably be asking her out," Diana said. "I mean, she's pretty and she certainly seems to like you."

"No reason why I can't date all of them, is there?" Bart asked. "I'm not ready to settle for one girl, not when there are so many here to help me forget the girl I left behind."

"Which girl you left behind?" Diana asked.

Bart's eyes flashed with laughter as he tried to look sad. "Does it matter when you have a broken heart that needs healing?" he asked, as they went inside.

"Honestly, Bart, you are. . . ."

"There you are," their mother called from the living room. "I was beginning to think you'd gotten lost. Your father just called and he'll be home in about an hour. Come and tell me all about the kids you met."

Diana swallowed a sigh, suddenly wishing that she could just go to her room and unpack some of the things she'd brought from the ranch. She had a strong urge to make her room a haven from the newness of everything around her.

Their mother seemed pleased with everything they told her.

"I just hope this doesn't mean that you two are going to be spending all your time with your dates and activities," Rose said as Diana and Bart headed for their rooms to get ready for dinner. "I mean, one of the reasons we decided to move to Rose Hill was so we could have some time together as a family."

"Gee, Mom, we're going to be here for dinner," Bart teased.

"You're terrible," she told him, laughing, "but I'm glad to have you anyway. Your father hasn't been around much lately, so maybe having you two here will make him remember he has a family to spend time with."

"I'm sure we'll both be around plenty, Mom," Diana said, trying to make her mother feel better. She certainly hadn't seemed too happy since they arrived in Rose Hill.

"Don't count on it," Bart told her. "That John Marquette was really impressed with you. I'll bet he asks you out again before you get to the riding stable."

Diana just laughed, but she had a feeling he might be right. Well, she was looking forward to it. She'd never had a serious boyfriend that she could count on for dates to school dances and parties. Maybe she would in Rose Hill. That wouldn't be a bad start to a new school year.

"Not only does she have a big football hero interested, but there's this guy from England who wants to photograph her," Bart continued. "My sister, the model."

"Oh, come on. Jeremy was just being friendly," Diana protested modestly. But she got that tingly feeling again just at the mention of his name. "He's new here, too," she told her mother.

"He was flirting with you," Bart teased. "He was watching you the whole time we were there. That was probably his line. 'Come out with me, pretty girl, I want to take your picture.'" He posed on the stairs with an imaginary camera, pretending to snap her picture as she playfully aimed a blow at him.

Still giggling at her brother, Diana ran up the stairs without another word. She could hardly believe so much had happened after just one afternoon in Rose Hill.

"What's the matter, Sash?" Phoebe asked as the two girls walked along the street toward Phoebe's house.

"I was just thinking about John and the new girl," Sasha said. "Do you think I should have told her what he tried with me?"

Phoebe sighed. "I thought about it, too," she admitted, "but he acted so different. And it is just a riding date and he did invite her brother along, so. . . ." She let her words trail off.

"He had been drinking that night he made a pass at me," Sasha said, frowning. "I'd just feel awful if he did anything to scare or hurt Diana. She seems really nice."

"You could call her," Phoebe suggested.

"But what if he really has changed?" Sasha asked. "If he is serious about Diana, maybe I could ruin everything for him. Woody said Ted seemed to think he had changed. I just find it hard to believe after what I went through with him." Sasha had practically been blackmailed into interviewing John Marquette for the school paper. He had insisted that they conduct the interview in his cousin's apartment, then refused to let Sasha leave once they got there.

"You're right. He probably couldn't contain the deep uncontrollable passion he had for you," Phoebe teased, though she knew her friend was truly troubled.

"Maybe I should tell Bart tomorrow, just so he'll be on the lookout for his sister. He'll know how she feels about John, and he can decide whether or not Diana should know. What do you think?"

Phoebe considered, then nodded. "I think that's the best idea. Since he's a football player, he'll probably get to know John better than the rest of us, so that should help, too. I don't think even Marquette would be dumb enough to play rough with the sister of a guy like Bart Einerson."

"He is a gorgeous addition to the neighborhood, isn't he?" Sasha said. "But such a flirt."

"You noticed." They giggled together, then Phoebe sobered a little. "What do you think about

Gloria showing up with him?" she asked.

"Oh, I have a feeling she singled him out and had the great idea of bringing him to meet us to see if we've forgiven her. I still have bad feelings for her after what she pulled last year," Sasha said.

Phoebe sighed. "Yeah, so do I. But it's pretty hard to think about last year when we're just about to start our senior year. Can you believe it, Sash?" she asked. "We're finally going to be seniors. It's our last year at Kennedy High."

"It's a scary thought," Sasha added, "but I'm pretty excited. I never thought I'd be so anxious for school to start, but right now I can hardly wait."

"Me, either. See you tomorrow, Sasha," Phoebe said, as the girls headed their separate ways.

Chapter
3

By a quarter to one on Saturday afternoon, Diana was a quivering bundle of nerves. She'd tried on every shirt and pair of pants she owned and had redone her hair three times. She finally settled on a simple brown-and-orange-plaid shirt, and brown jeans secured by a tooled leather belt with an engraved copper buckle that had been a gift from her best friend Barbara.

"I should never have accepted this date," she told her reflection in the dressing table mirror, as she tied an orange scarf around her ponytail and studied the effect. What had Jeremy seen? she asked herself. She just wasn't used to so much attention.

The doorbell sounded and she stiffened. It had to be John. Suddenly she couldn't remember what he looked like. He was practically a stranger. She had a stomach full of butterflies.

"Diana, John's here," her mother called.

"I'll be right down," she replied, swallowing the lump in her throat. She took several deep breaths before she touched a bit of coral lipstick to her mouth and gave her hair a final pat. It was too late now to back out.

John's wide smile greeted her as she came down the stairs and she sensed immediately that her mother approved of him. "Don't you look pretty," he said. "Like a real cowgirl."

"I am a real cowgirl," Diana reminded him. "I've ridden on roundups since I was eight."

"Oh, by the way, Diana," her mother said, "your father just called to say that we've been invited to a cocktail party, so I probably won't be here when you get home from riding."

"If it's all right with you, Mrs. Einerson, I'd like your permission to take Diana out for pizza or a hamburger, then maybe to a movie," John said. "If you'd like to go, Diana." His eyes met hers and he was no longer a stranger, just the friendly boy she'd met at the sub shop — one who made her feel special.

"Well, sure, that sounds like fun," she said. "If it's okay with you, Mom?"

"Sure," her mother said. "If we aren't going to be here for dinner and Bart isn't either, there's no reason why you should have to eat alone."

"Bart won't be home?" Diana was surprised.

Her mother laughed. "Do you really think he won't have made some plans for the evening?"

"It is Saturday night," Diana agreed. "Well, have fun at the cocktail party."

"And you two enjoy your good ride."

Once they were in the car, Diana became uncomfortable again. She was conscious of John's admiring gaze and it disturbed her as much as her inability to think of anything to say. At home she'd always known her dates for years and they'd had school assignments or activities to discuss.

"Your mom is nice," John said.

"I think she liked you, too," Diana said.

"She knew she could trust me to take care of you," John stated. "I mean, this is a new area for you, so you need someone to show you around, help you get acquainted."

Diana wasn't sure she agreed with his rather arrogant assessment so she decided to change the subject. "Tell me about your sister's riding stable," she began. "Do you go there a lot?"

John grinned at her. "The truth is, I don't come often. Riding and showing horses was always Irene's big thing, not mine. I didn't get interested in riding until this summer."

"Oh." The admission made her a bit skeptical. "You do like to ride, don't you?" she asked after a few minutes of silence.

"I wouldn't lie about that, Diana," he said. His gaze was very level and honest. "I had a great time at camp. They had me counseling a younger group of boys, and I took them out on the trails every day. They really depended on me and I did my best to get them into shape. It was a blast."

The pride in his voice made her smile, and she began to look forward to a pleasant afternoon of riding.

Picturesque Danberry Stable was an unexpected delight. White clapboard buildings with red roofs and neat white-fenced paddocks were spread out on both sides of the narrow road. A half-dozen riders were milling around, some in an arena where there were low jumps for the horses, others heading into the green meadows that rolled away on three sides of the buildings. John parked the car and opened the door for her before waving to a stocky brunette, who was just emerging from one of the stables.

"Hey, Irene, come here," he called.

"You must be Diana," Irene said, offering her hand. "John tells me that you're from Montana."

"Hello, Mrs. . . ?" Diana colored slightly at this proof of John's interest in her.

"Just call me Irene," Irene Danberry said. "What do you think of the place?"

"It looks like a beautiful place to ride," Diana said. "I was so excited when I heard there was a stable so close to Rose Hill. It's only been a few days, but it seems like years since I've been on a horse."

"We can certainly remedy that," Irene told her. "I've always got horses that need exercise. It's just too bad school's starting so soon. I could have used your help this summer. People board horses here and don't ride more than a couple of times a month. Horses need exercise every day."

"Don't let her get started, Diana," John warned. "We'll never get to ride. She'll show you every horse on the place and give you their bloodlines and show records and. . . ."

"Diana would know what I was talking about, which is more than I can say for you, little brother," Irene said with a grin that made Diana feel at home. "But he's right, I'll save the grand tour and equine introductions for your next visit, Diana. Right now I have a couple of horses saddled and waiting for you."

The horses were better than Diana had dared hope and she was relieved to see that they bore Western saddles since many of the riders here were using English tack. The two geldings snorted and danced when they mounted, and Diana was pleased to see that John knew how to handle the big black horse he was riding.

"Any place special we should ride, Sis?" John asked, after they'd walked and trotted the two horses around the stableyard a few times.

"You might try the ridge trail," Irene suggested. "It's pretty out that way and you could check on Galaxy for me. She and her filly are in that pasture."

John rolled his eyes, but nodded. "This way, Diana," he said. "We'll help Sis by playing mother hen for her favorite horse."

"I have a right to worry about her," Irene called after them. "She's an old mare and that's a special foal."

"I don't mind checking for her," Diana assured him. "I know what it's like to worry about horses. I hope they're taking good care of my Appaloosas at the Lazy E."

"Your what?" John asked.

Diana relaxed and happily began to describe her small herd of exotically spotted horses. She felt at home here and she was getting comfortable with John's company. He didn't seem too different from the boys she'd dated back home.

"You know, this is really great," he said as

they trotted through the trees and crossed a small stream that meandered along the base of the ridge. "I've never met anyone like you, Diana. You're so different from that crowd you were with yesterday. All those girls make smart cracks and show off."

"Oh, come on. I thought everyone was really nice," Diana protested, thinking especially of Janie and remembering that most of the group didn't seem too fond of John.

"They were all flirting with your brother. They really go for football players. I mean, who wouldn't after hanging around with guys like Woody and Peter and Henry? What kind of guys are more interested in clothes and music and putting on shows than they are in doing stuff like riding and wrestling and playing football?"

"Are you a wrestler, too, John?" Diana asked, preferring not to try to answer his question.

"State-ranked," John answered proudly. "My dad says I'm sure to get an athletic scholarship for most any college I want."

"You and Bart have a lot in common," Diana said. "He's very good in sports, too. In fact, he was. . . ." She stopped as she heard a sound in the distance.

"What's the matter, Diana?" John asked, concerned.

"I thought I heard something." She strained her ears. The bay she was riding snorted and turned his head, his ears pricked sharply forward as though he was listening for the same sounds. When she heard the sounds again, Diana kicked the bay into a gallop and rode toward it. She was barely conscious that John was racing after her.

They reached the top of the ridge and reined in, looking down through the trees. There was a narrow ravine winding along the bottom of the slope below and a white horse was pacing wildly back and forth through the trees, whinnying frantically.

"That must be Galaxy," John gasped as they both urged their horses off the trail and down the hill as fast as they dared.

The old white mare stopped as they approached and even in her lathered and dirty state, Diana could see that she'd been a magnificent animal. Now she was limping and her head drooped when she stood still. A squeal came from beyond the thick hedge of brush that rimmed the ravine and the mare reacted as though spurred, pacing and whinnying.

"What's the matter with her?" John asked as he stopped his horse beside Diana's. "She looks crazy."

"Didn't your sister say Galaxy had a foal?" Diana asked.

"Yeah, I think so. Why?"

"Something must have happened to it." Diana dismounted and tied her horse to the nearest tree. She took the rope off the side of her saddle and said, "I'm going to catch the mare and see if I can calm her down. You take a look on the other side of those bushes and see if you can find the foal."

The mare was easy to catch, gentle even in her

terrible anxiety. Diana knotted the rope through the halter ring, then looked up as John came back through the brush.

"It's in the ravine," he said. "Just over there in the rocks."

"Tie the mare beside my horse," Diana said, handing him the rope, "and try to calm her down."

For just a moment, she saw something like anger flare in his dark eyes. Then it was gone and he took the rope. Diana pushed her way through the brush and stopped. The filly was right below her, caught in a narrow part of the ravine.

The tumbled rocks told the tale. The foal had fallen and landed on her back in a cleft in the rocks. Unable to turn over so she could get up, she'd been trapped and now was exhausted from her struggles. Diana leaned over and the foal's long legs stirred, but it was plain that she was weak and couldn't last much longer.

"What should we do?" John asked, joining her.

Diana frowned, concentrating. "If we could get a rope around the front half of her, we might be able to use one of the horses to pull her out. She might be badly injured from the fall, but if she isn't, we could save her by getting her on her feet."

"I can get the rope around her," John said.

"She's heavy and she's wedged herself in pretty tight," Diana warned. "And she's liable to fight us, too."

John shrugged. "We can't just leave her there. She looks awful."

Diana had to agree. Bringing help would take close to an hour and she had a strong hunch the filly wouldn't last that long. Horses weren't meant to lie on their backs and her struggling had taken a heavy toll. "Your horse is bigger than the one I'm riding," she said. "Give me your rope, then take the horse down into the ravine where the sides aren't so steep."

Again she sensed a resistance to taking her orders, but after a moment John did as she asked, and she turned her attention to the stricken filly. The trapped horse began to struggle the moment Diana came close, so she took off her scarf and tied it gently around the slender head, covering the white-ringed brown eyes. The sudden darkness froze the filly and kept her still as John left his horse to come to her aid.

"What we need to do is to get the rope around her body the way a saddle cinch would go, then run it across her chest to hold it. Once it's in place, I'll tie the other end to your saddle horn and we'll use your horse to pull her up on her haunches. Do you think you can steady her enough to keep her from breaking a leg when she turns over?" Diana asked. "I'd do it, but I don't think I'm strong enough and she'd end up falling on me."

"I can handle it," John said. "But will it work?"

"We won't know until we try it." Diana gave him a hopeful smile. "I don't have any other ideas, though, do you? She's too heavy even for two of us to lift."

It was back-breaking work, but after a couple of tries, John finally lifted the filly enough for

Diana to slip the rope past the sharp bump of her withers. Diana drew it around the bony ribs, knotted it, then made the chest loop and knotted that so it wouldn't slip and tighten on the foal. She carried the loose end of the rope and secured it to the big black horse's saddle horn.

"Okay, John, as the horse pulls her up on her haunches, you'll have to move in behind her and keep her balanced. She'll probably panic, so if you can jerk the blindfold off just as she goes over on her belly, that might help to distract her. Horses can only think of one thing at a time, and suddenly being able to see again should calm her."

"I hope you know what you're doing," he said as she mounted the big black gelding.

"So do I," she replied. "Are you ready?"

"Let's go." He squatted behind the filly's head and Diana began urging the horse forward slowly, feeling the rope tightening under her leg. She would have preferred a well-trained cowpony like the ones she'd had in Montana, but the gelding was strong and well-behaved. He snorted when the rope pulled the saddle back, but he continued to move ahead slowly.

Diana held her breath as the filly's chestnut body rose out of the rocky crevice and John moved in to wrap his big arms around her, holding her steady as she was pulled up on her haunches. For a moment she teetered on her rump, then abruptly she dropped forward. John's reflexes were perfect. He released his hold and jerked the scarf off the filly's eyes just as she landed on her feet.

For a few seconds, the foal struggled, then she collapsed and Diana's heart sank to the ground with her. She stopped the gelding and freed the rope before she dismounted. The filly was quivering and panting, her thin legs spraddled out.

"What's the matter with her?" John demanded, joining Diana.

Diana shrugged. "I have no idea. She may have hurt her back in the fall. We'll just have to give her a few minutes, then see if she tries to get up."

The few minutes seemed to last forever, and Diana was glad when John's warm hand clasped her cold one. She felt sick at the idea that they might have come too late to save the filly, yet she knew that they'd had to try. Suddenly the air was torn by the filly's frantic whinny.

For a couple of heartbeats nothing happened, then the filly began to struggle. Her legs didn't seem to work quite right, but gradually she mastered them and made it to her feet, swaying drunkenly as she squealed an answer to her mother. Diana moved quickly to untie the harness they'd fashioned with the rope.

"Is she okay?" John asked.

"She can stand," Diana said, then laughed with relief as the filly took her first steps. "And walk!" she crowed. "We did it, John. She's going to be all right."

John's hug nearly crushed the breath from her lungs, but she didn't mind; she hugged him back with all the joy she felt.

Suddenly John released his hold to a more gentle one. Diana found herself looking straight into his dark eyes. He looked very serious as he bent his head closer to hers. They both were tingling with excitement after the adventure with the horses. Something about the dramatic rescue had heightened their feelings and Diana felt strongly drawn to John.

Their lips met in a slow and gentle kiss that sent shivers down her spine. She pressed her body closer to his, enjoying the secure feel of his strong arms around her.

Chapter
4

Gloria put on her best smile as she entered the sub shop. She knew Sasha and Bart would be there and she had no intention of letting the two of them get too close. Besides, she couldn't afford to miss any opportunity to cement her relationship with the group. Bringing Bart and Diana to meet them had been a start, but she knew she wasn't really welcome yet. She swallowed her doubts and sauntered over to the table where they were gathered.

"Hi everyone. What's new?" she asked, looking around expectantly.

"We were just drinking a soda to the end of summer," Woody said.

"And the beginning of our senior year," Phoebe added. "I keep telling myself that this will be my last year at Kennedy, and I still can't believe it."

"Yeah, you're lucky," Gloria murmured. "I

wish it was my last year. You must feel wonderful."

"Who's wonderful?" Bart asked, looking around and grinning at her. "Hi, Gloria, I didn't see you come in."

"Are you finished with your interview?" Gloria asked, giving him a special, high-voltage smile.

"Yeah, we just finished. I thought I'd better leave a few stories for Diana to tell," Bart said.

Just then Jeremy Stone walked in.

"Ah, you're the person I've been waiting for," Woody said, with a theatrical leer.

"Should I turn around and run?" Jeremy said with a grin that lit up his whole face. "What have I done to deserve all this attention?"

"It's what you might be going to do," Woody informed him. "I have some interesting news. My mom was talking with a guy from Kennedy High's theater arts department last night and he told her they just got the funds to offer a class on video production. They're going to let people add it to their schedules."

"Like music videos?" Peter asked.

Woody shrugged. "I don't have any details, but I figured a resident photography buff would be interested."

"He's not the only one," Peter said. "This sounds great, don't you think, Jeremy? We could make a fantastic music video."

Everyone turned to face Jeremy, who looked like he was about to explode with excitement. "It sounds smashing." he said.

"I can just see it all now," Phoebe said, giggling. "A great plot written by the brilliant Sasha

Jenkins, music edited by star DJ Peter Lacey, filmed by internationally renowned movie maker Jeremy Stone, and directed by our own Woody Webster, who loves to order people around more than anything else in the world."

"Pheeberooni, you are so hard on me. You know all I do is make suggestions, never give orders," Woody joked back.

"And don't forget Henry for costumes," Gloria added, "and Bart can play the hero with the rest of us as supporting cast."

"Gee, and I thought you guys would like the idea," Woody said with a sad face. "Oh, well, I suppose someone else will want to try it."

Everyone laughed, then Jeremy looked at Bart. "Do you think your sister would like to be in it?" he asked, then blushed as everyone looked at him quizzically.

"Still wanting to take her picture?" Bart teased, then shrugged. "I don't know about Diana," he admitted. "You'll have to ask her yourself."

"Where is she?" Jeremy looked around.

"She went horseback riding with John Marquette," Phoebe said. "I guess he asked her before you came in yesterday."

Gloria watched Jeremy with interest. She'd seen him a couple of times before, but she hadn't really noticed how attractive he was. If Jeremy was going to be the one making the video. . . . She smiled at him. Perhaps they should become better friends. After all, he was new in Rose Hill and he was a junior, too. If things didn't work out with Bart, it would be nice to have someone else to date.

Diana smoothed her brown linen skirt over her hips and checked the back of her beige cotton blouse. With her long blonde hair up in a French twist, she looked years older and more sophisticated than the girl who'd gone riding with John Marquette this afternoon. After the scene at the riding stable, she felt nervous all over again about seeing him. It was obvious he had strong feelings for her, and she wasn't at all sure how she felt about him.

"I wish Bart would get home," she murmured to herself as she paced around the living room again.

She and John had stayed at the Danberry Stable with Galaxy and her foal until after the veterinarian had examined them both and pronounced them sound, though exhausted. He'd been very lavish with his praise.

"These two saved the foal for sure and probably the mare as well. Another half hour out there and Galaxy would have collapsed from stress and exhaustion. As it is, you'll need to keep them in for a couple of weeks, just to be safe."

Irene and her husband Jack Danberry were extremely grateful to Diana and encouraged her to come back and ride any time she wanted to. Diana was happy, too, that she'd made some new friends, and she looked forward to seeing them again.

She sighed. "So why am I having cold feet?" she asked herself. "John was terrific today. He's a great guy and we're going to have a wonderful time tonight." Her thoughts were interrupted by the sound of a car in the drive and she ran to the window just in time to see Bart getting out of the station wagon. She hurried to open the door, glad to have someone to talk to.

"Well, well, you don't look like someone planning to stay home and heat up a frozen dinner," Bart commented as he came in. "Don't tell me the big man is taking you out for dinner, too?"

"Okay, I won't tell you," Diana responded, feeling better in spite of his teasing — or maybe because of it. She and Bart had a good relationship, even though he did love to torment her. "What have you been up to? Is your broken heart just about mended?"

"I spent some time with Sasha doing the interview and she really seems nice. Everyone we met yesterday was at the sub shop again. You and John should have come in after your ride. Jeremy was asking for you."

"Are you serious?" Diana asked, not sure whether or not to believe him.

"They were all talking about some video class that's going to be offered for the first time this year and he wanted to know if you'd be in it," Bart explained.

"In what?"

"The video, dummy." Bart shook his head. "We're supposed to meet them tomorrow to talk more about it."

"We?" Diana repeated.

"You were definitely included in the invitation," Bart assured her.

"Oh, I don't know," Diana began, then was

interrupted by the doorbell. "That must be John," she said. "Will you let him in? I have to go up and get my jacket."

"Take your time," Bart said. "I want to talk to him about the football team."

"Just don't forget that he's here to see *me*," Diana teased as she ran up the stairs.

John and Bart were deep in conversation when she came back down. When they looked up, she saw the sheepish expression on Bart's face even before John said, "I hope you don't mind, Diana, but I told Bart he could come out to dinner with us since he doesn't have any other plans."

"That's okay," Diana said, caught between amusement and irritation. "Want to go to the movie, too, Bart?" she joked.

"No way," he said, grinning at her. "Don't worry. I'll find a way to amuse myself so you two can watch the movie all by yourselves."

"You'd better leave a note for the folks," Diana warned. "Mom knows where I'm going, but they'll be wondering about you."

After Bart left the room to find a pencil and paper, John fumbled awkwardly in his pocket. "This is for you, Diana." He held out a small box wrapped in silver paper.

"Oh, John. . . ." Diana didn't know what to say as she accepted the gift.

"Why don't you open it?" John said.

Diana's fingers were clumsy as she pulled off the paper and lifted the lid. Inside were two small porcelain figures — a dainty white mare and a tiny chestnut-colored foal. "Galaxy and her baby," Diana gasped, delighted by the gift. "Oh, John, they're wonderful. Thank you so much."

"I hope every time you look at them, you'll think of our afternoon together," he said. "Now, are you ready to go?"

Diana nodded as Bart came back into the room. He saw the box, and she and John spent most of their time at dinner telling him in great detail about the rescue of the filly. By the time they parted outside the restaurant, she felt comfortable with John again and was happy to be spending the evening with him.

The movie was an engrossing thriller and Diana didn't mind when John slipped an arm around her shoulders. He didn't laugh at her when she screamed and hid her eyes during the gory parts; he just tightened his protective hold and patted her shoulder. It was a nice change from the teasing she always got from the boys she was used to dating.

As he drove her home through the still unfamiliar streets of Rose Hill, John grinned at her. "This has been a really special day, Diana," he began, "and I'd like to take you out again."

"I'd like that, too," she responded shyly.

"I have to go to a family picnic tomorrow and school starts on Monday, but how about next Saturday night? The Danberry Stable is sponsoring a benefit hayride and cookout and I'd love to go with you. Will you come?"

"That sounds great! I haven't been on a hayride in years. I'd love to go."

"It's a date then," John said. "I'll have to find

out from Irene what time they leave and everything, but we'll see each other at school on Monday." He sighed. "I wish I could take you out during the week, but with football practice starting and my job at Superjock, I don't have much free time."

"I'm not sure Mom would let me go out on a school night anyway," Diana admitted. "At least not at first. Starting in at a new school is going to be kind of hard. There'll be a lot to get used to."

"You'll do great," John assured her, "and if anybody gives you any trouble, you just tell me and I'll make sure they leave you alone."

"Thanks," Diana said, managing not to giggle at the solemn way John seemed to be setting himself up as her protector. She didn't want to hurt his feelings by assuring him she was perfectly capable of taking care of herself.

John acted almost shy as he walked her to the door. He took both her hands in his as they stood on the front porch. "I guess I'll see you at school on Monday," he said. "Maybe we can eat lunch together. The school food is bad news, so you'd better bring something from home."

Diana giggled. "Some things are the same everywhere. I never liked anything they cooked at our cafeteria in Helena either."

"I'm glad you're here and not there," John said, then looked embarrassed as he gave her a quick peck on the cheek and fled. Diana felt a little disappointed that it was nothing like the kiss they'd shared that afternoon, but she figured that the earlier kiss had had as much to do with events that had preceded it as it did with the way John felt about her.

Diana called her thanks after him, then started to unlock the door. It opened before she could get the key in the lock and Bart smiled at her. "Have a good time?" he asked.

"Great," Diana said. "How about you?"

"Fantastic," Bart answered. "This isn't such a bad town and it is filled with absolutely beautiful women!" He looked pleased with himself as he settled down with a glass of milk and began to tell Diana about his evening. "You and John should have come with me," he said. "I went to the sub shop and met a lot of people from school."

"A lot of girls, you mean," Diana teased.

"Well, I did meet Laurie Bennington and she is gorgeous. Also beautiful, blonde Chris Austin — who recently broke up with the football team quarterback, Ted Mason. She's supposedly got a new boyfriend, but I hear this guy's only a sophomore."

"Ah," Diana said.

"She has a stepsister named Brenda who's pretty foxy, too. And Gloria, Phoebe, and Sasha were there, too."

"Sounds like fun," Diana said. "I'm happy my big brother is already so popular."

"You're not doing so bad yourself," Bart said. "How was your date after we parted?"

"John's really very nice," Diana murmured. "And he asked me out for next weekend, too."

"Like I said," Bart observed, "moving here

wasn't such a bad idea. I think I might end up liking it. I'm going to bed before I fall asleep on the table. 'Night, Diana."

I think I'm going to like it, too, Diana thought to herself as she followed Bart up the stairs.

Chapter
5

"Are you sure I'm really supposed to be going with you?" Diana asked for the third time Sunday afternoon.

Bart glared at her. "If I'd known you wanted an engraved invitation, I would have asked for one."

"I'm sorry," Diana said. "I just feel a little strange. I haven't even met most of the group and now everyone is going to that girl's house instead of the sub shop."

"That girl is Laurie Bennington. I told you, I met her last night and she's very nice, so would you quit worrying?"

"Why is everyone going to her place, anyway?" Diana asked.

"To talk about this video they want to make for school. According to Henry, Laurie's father owns the most successful cable TV station in

D.C., and he has all this fancy equipment. She invited everyone over to eat lunch and watch some new videos for ideas."

Diana raised her eyebrows at him. "I didn't know you were so interested in video productions."

His grin was wicked. "I'm interested in the people who are interested in video productions," he replied, then sobered a little. "It's something you should consider, too, Diana," he advised. "This isn't Helena. If you want to be a part of things here, you're going to have to be interested in more than riding horses."

"Well, I am, but. . . ." Diana began.

"Besides, Janie and Henry are picking us up, and Janie definitely asked if you were coming along."

"I liked her," Diana admitted, warming to the idea of going.

"And Jeremy will be there, too," Bart continued. "He was asking about you last night and wanted to be sure you were coming today." He chuckled. "I think he's as smitten with you as big John."

They were suddenly interrupted by the doorbell. "Is that them already?" she asked Bart as he peered out the window.

"No, it's Gloria. She's coming, too, and probably wants a ride."

"I'd say you've made a conquest," Diana teased as he went to answer the door. Bart flashed her a wide grin.

"Oh, hi, Diana," Gloria said, looking surprised to see her. "I thought you'd be out with John."

"He's at a family picnic today," Diana answered.

"Then are you going to the sub shop with us?" Gloria asked, not looking pleased at the prospect.

"The plans have changed," Bart informed her. "Henry called about half an hour ago and we're going to Laurie Bennington's instead."

"How did Laurie get involved in this?" Gloria asked, looking even less enthusiastic.

"The video project." Bart explained that they were going to Laurie's to watch videos. "Do you want to ride along with us?" he finished.

"Well, if you're sure they won't mind," Gloria said, with what looked to Diana like genuine reluctance. Diana couldn't help wondering what was troubling her. Gloria definitely seemed hesitant to go to Laurie Bennington's house, and Diana wondered why. She had little time to think about it, however, for Henry and Janie arrived almost immediately.

Diana didn't miss Gloria's flash of anger as Bart eased her into the back seat with Diana, then settled himself in the front next to Janie.

"I'm so glad you could come today, Diana," Janie said. "This video project really sounds like it's going to be fun."

"Are you going to sign up for the class?" Diana asked.

"I don't think so," Janie admitted, "but if the guys do decide they want Henry to do the costumes for their video, I'll be involved."

"It would be fun to help out, but I don't know what I could do," Diana said. "Horseback riding is more my style."

"Maybe they'll decide to do a Western," Gloria observed.

"If Jeremy has his way, they might," Bart agreed. "He is obsessed with cowboys and cattle drives and ranching. You'll have to offer to take him riding, Diana, he'd probably love it."

Diana blushed, not sure why she felt such mixed emotions at the idea. There was something so unsettling about Jeremy. She was glad when Gloria began teasing Bart about starring in a Western, so she didn't have to say anything about Jeremy.

The Benningtons' house was grand with its big rooms and huge pool in the backyard, but Diana didn't feel much at home there. Laurie was pleasant when they were introduced, but it was obvious that she was more interested in impressing everyone with her father's equipment than being friends, so Diana was glad when Janie drew her to one side.

"How was your date with John yesterday? Was he nice to you?" Janie asked.

"He was sweet," Diana said, disturbed by the question.

"Sweet? John Marquette?" Janie looked dubious. "That's hard to believe."

"Why?"

"I'm sorry to sound so suspicious. It's just that he gave Sasha a very hard time when he took her out last winter, and he hasn't exactly ever been nice to me." Janie's level gaze was too honest to hide malice.

"But he was just wonderful to me," Diana said, then described her day with the big wrestler. "He treats me like a princess, really, and he wasn't a bit rough — just very gentle and sweet."

Janie shook her head. "Wow! That's incredible, Diana. Maybe you're what he needs. It sounds like he's turned over a new leaf. But you should still be careful, just in case, okay?"

"Well, sure, but. . . ." She didn't know what to say. John seemed like a perfectly nice guy to her. Suddenly she looked up and found herself facing Jeremy. He was so handsome it took her breath away, and for a moment, time seemed to stand still. Then Gloria moved between them, and Diana was back in the real world again.

"We've been waiting for you, Jeremy," Gloria said. "Have you come up with any ideas for the video?"

He swallowed hard and looked away from Diana to smile at Gloria. "I don't think we can make any plans until we find out what the class requirements are," he said.

"But you're our expert," Gloria protested with a pout. "You must have some ideas."

"Why don't we look at the videos Daddy brought home for me?" Laurie suggested. "Maybe they'll give you some ideas, Jeremy."

"Sounds like a good plan," Jeremy said, easing away from Gloria and managing to reach Diana's side before the first video started on the big screen. He sat down on the couch beside her, far more conscious of brushing against Diana's creamy skin than he was of the images on the screen.

"Hi," Diana whispered, smiling at him in a way that made his heartbeat quicken.

"I didn't know if you'd come," he said, "but I'm glad you're here. I hope this means you want to be in our video."

"Well, the video sounds interesting," Diana replied, "but I don't know a thing about making movies."

"It doesn't matter. You can still be in it," Jeremy assured her. "I just wish you'd let me take your picture, Diana. Then I can show you what I mean. I have a feeling you're extremely photogenic and I know you'd agree once you see your picture."

"Well, uh . . ." Diana began, looking up at him. "I guess I could agree to being in the video. It would be a good way to get to know everybody."

"Great," Jeremy said. "Now tell me all about that famous rescue I've heard so much about. And then I want to hear all about Montana. I'd love to see the West."

His enthusiasm was contagious and Diana found herself relaxing as she told the story of the rescue of Galaxy and her foal once again. From there the conversation moved easily to what life on the ranch was like, and then she told him all about their family trip to Disneyland and Hollywood the previous summer. He asked a million questions and listened intently to everything she said.

"Did you take pictures?" he asked.

"Tons," Diana answered. "They're not great, but I got a camera for my birthday last year and decided to put together an album from the trip."

"Could I see it sometime?" Jeremy asked. "I mean, I don't know if I'll ever get to Hollywood and I'd love to see what a studio backlot looks like."

"Well, sure," Diana said, "but I don't think you'll be too impressed. I mean, I'm not a real photographer like you are, and my pictures are just snapshots."

"Oh, come on, Diana, I'd really like to see them. Let's make it an official date," he suggested. "Phoebe's going to have a 'Farewell to Summer' party at the Halls' mountain cabin next Friday night. Would you go with me?"

"Oh, Jeremy, I'd love to," she said. She felt the heat rising in her cheeks, and when she looked at him she felt a rush of excitement.

"Terrific," he said. She could sense his relief and could barely believe he had thought she might say no.

"It takes about an hour to get to the Halls' cabin, so that's plenty of time for me to talk you into letting me photograph you." He gave her hand a gentle squeeze. Diana felt her face grow hot again as she realized that the videos were over and everyone was looking at them, waiting for Jeremy's reaction.

"So what do you think, Jeremy?" Woody asked. "What are we going to do to prove we're the real geniuses at Kennedy?"

Jeremy didn't answer at first. Then he was quickly drawn into the conversation as everyone began to offer ideas for how they could make the best video.

But Diana could barely pay attention. She leaned back against the couch with a sigh, remembering the way her hand felt resting in

Jeremy's. Her fingers were still warm from that sudden handclasp, and her heart was beating fast. She felt dizzy and light-headed and surprisingly happy. She was so excited that Jeremy had asked her out. A date with Jeremy Friday night, and one with John on Saturday.

"Hi, Diana. How was your afternoon with John yesterday?" someone asked from behind her. Diana turned to see Sasha standing beside the couch. "Did it go okay?"

"I'm getting a little tired of everyone implying that John's not such a nice guy," Diana said, her pleasure suddenly fading. "He's been really great to me and I don't know why everyone keeps warning me about him." She jumped to her feet and ran out to the backyard. Once there, however, she had nowhere to go and as her brief flare of temper died down, she began to be sorry she'd snapped at Sasha. She wandered around the pool and sat down by the edge, peering over at her reflection.

What was the matter with her? she asked herself. Why had she gotten so angry at Sasha? Janie had told her about Sasha's bad experience with John, and Sasha was only trying to be a friend. Now she really felt awful. The memory of Jeremy holding her hand had faded so abruptly, it seemed like nothing would bring back the good feeling. These kids were just trying to be friendly and here she was lashing out at them. But maybe something else was beneath these feelings. Why had her own warm feelings toward John disappeared so quickly as she sat and talked with Jeremy?

"Diana?" Sasha came up and put a hand on her shoulder. "Could I talk to you?"

Diana nodded, feeling both relieved and embarrassed.

"I'm sorry, Diana. I should have been more straightforward with you about what happened between me and John Marquette. But if he's really changed and he treats you well, I should be willing to give him the benefit of the doubt. I just didn't want someone as nice as you to be hurt the way I nearly was. Okay?"

"I'm sorry, too," Diana said, finding her voice. "I really don't know John very well and I do appreciate the fact that you care enough to warn me. He was very nice to me yesterday and he asked me to go on a hayride with him next Saturday night, and I said yes."

"A hayride? Is it the benefit at Danberry Stable?" Sasha asked.

"Yes," Diana answered. "It's to raise money for riding classes for handicapped kids."

"I've heard about it. It sounds like fun," Sasha said. "Have you told anyone else? It sounds like the kind of thing Jeremy would be really interested in doing. Maybe a bunch of us could go."

"That would be great," Diana agreed. "I can't get over how friendly everyone has been. I expected it to be so hard. I wasn't particularly excited about starting a new school in my junior year, but you've all been terrific. I'm looking forward to getting to know everyone better at Phoebe's party Friday."

"Phoebe throws great parties," Sasha said, "and

it's so pretty up at the Halls' cabin. I think you're really going to like it."

"Hey, you two," Woody called from the back door, "Laurie ordered some pizzas from Mario's and they just arrived. You'd better come in and claim your slices or you won't get a bite."

"I hope she ordered an all vegetable," Sasha said as they headed for the house. "Vegetarian pizza is Laurie's idea of health food."

Diana started to ask Sasha why she was a vegetarian, but before she had a chance, Jeremy approached her and led her away by the hand. "I've been looking all over for you," he said. "I don't think you finished telling me what a cattle roundup is really like."

Diana smiled at him, feeling very much a part of the group as they crowded around the table and helped themselves to the hot pizza.

Chapter
6

The first few days of school were so hectic, Diana began to wish she could clone a twin to handle the overload. She got lost in the rush between classes, had trouble remembering where her locker was, and was overwhelmed by how different the subjects seemed from the ones she'd taken last year in Helena.

The one constant in the chaos was John, but Diana wasn't sure whether to be grateful for his attention or frustrated that he was separating her from all the activity around her. He somehow managed to be waiting for her outside her last morning class each day and he insisted on walking her to her locker to get her lunch, then eating with her on the quad or in the lunchroom. The first few days she'd been pleased, but by Thursday it was beginning to seem a little stifling.

"We're going riding after school," he informed

her as they spread out their lunches on what was rapidly becoming "their" table. "I called Irene and made all the arrangements."

"Don't you think you should have asked me first?" Diana asked. "What if I've made other plans?"

"Have you?" John looked so stunned she almost forgot to be angry with him.

"Well, no, but. . . ."

"So don't you want to go riding?" he asked. "You said yesterday that you were sorry our ride was cut short on Saturday, so I thought as long as I wasn't going to be tied up after school today, it would be a good time to go."

"Well, of course I want to go riding, but. . . ." She let her words trail off, unable to explain her feelings when he was looking at her so adoringly. "I'd love to go riding, John," she told him, swallowing a sigh. "But I'll have to call Mom and make sure it's okay with her." She couldn't help feeling irritated with him. He was beginning to act like he owned her. He didn't even want to eat lunch with the rest of the gang and protested whenever she suggested it.

Diana unwrapped her sandwich and cast a longing glance at the laughing group in the corner. Then she noticed Jeremy entering the lunchroom. She smiled when he looked over at her and she had a sudden urge to be talking to him, instead of John. She knew she shouldn't be isolating herself like this and she made up her mind to eat with the group the next day, no matter what John said.

Jeremy walked over to Diana's table. "Hey, Diana," he said, "why don't you two eat with the rest of us? We've got some information on the video class now and we're starting to plan it."

She was relieved that someone else was suggesting they join the group so she wouldn't have to argue with John. Her dark eyes lit up as she smiled at Jeremy and started to get up.

"Hey, what's he talking about?" John asked, not even giving Jeremy a glance.

"The video class," Diana answered, her smile fading. "Everyone's been talking about it. Jeremy and Woody and Peter are going to make a video together and they've asked me to help. I thought it would be really interesting and I agreed."

"I haven't heard anything about it," Marquette growled, his expression darkening. "And I don't know why you'd want to help them."

"We talked about it last Sunday and I volunteered," Diana murmured, looking uncomfortable. She shuffled from one foot to the other, anxious to join the others and leave John behind. Jeremy began to regret his impetuous invitation.

"You shouldn't get involved in any dumb project with *that* crowd," John snorted. "We can find better things to do with our time, Diana."

She stood there with her mouth agape, too shocked by John's words to say anything.

"I think that should be Diana's decision," Jeremy intervened, his voice coming out louder that he had intended. "This is a pretty special project and I happen to think Diana would be great in it."

"Oh, you do, do you?" John was on his feet, towering ominously over Jeremy. "And just what business is it of yours, anyway, Stone? Diana is obviously with me, so why don't you just leave her alone?"

Jeremy stiffened, ready to do battle with the gigantic wrestler. The room had fallen silent suddenly and all eyes were turned their way.

"Cut it out, John," Diana said. "I told them I would be part of the project, and I intend to. You're really acting like a childish bully." With that she gathered up her lunch and purse and fled from the room without a backward glance.

Jeremy turned to follow her, but John's hand clamped down on his arm like a vise. "You stay out of this, creep," he rumbled. "That's my girl and she's going to listen to me." He shoved Jeremy hard into an empty chair and by the time Jeremy recovered, John had followed Diana from the lunchroom. Fighting fury, frustration, and embarrassment, Jeremy headed for his usual corner table.

Once outside, Diana hesitated, shivering as the cool breeze penetrated the thin cotton blouse she had on. She had been stupid to run outside, she thought furiously. Where was she going to go now? Then she felt a trickle of laughter welling up inside her. It was so awful, it was almost funny. What a scene!

"Diana?" She turned to see John standing in the doorway of the school. "Please come back. I'm sorry I made you mad."

For a moment she wanted to just walk away,

but his naughty puppy expression made her less angry. She almost felt sorry for him. "I guess I should have told you about the video project," she said, stepping in out of the wind.

"I just don't like you hanging around with that crowd," John said. "I don't trust that guy, and you aren't going to have time to get involved in any of their projects."

"I really want to do it," Diana said, not ready to yield to John's demand. "I think I'd learn a lot."

"You really want to do it?" He sounded surprised, and not too pleased.

"I'm going to talk to them more about it," Diana said, deciding that this wasn't the time to mention to John that she had a date with Jeremy the next night. "It's something I have to make up my own mind about, John."

He glared at her and she thought that he was going to continue to argue. Then his expression softened. "I just don't like to think of you doing things without me, Diana," he said. "I want us to share things like we did Saturday when we saved Galaxy's foal. We're a team, remember?"

"Of course I remember," Diana said, warming to his tender look.

"Come on in and call your mother about our going riding," he suggested.

"Don't you think it's going to be cold this afternoon?" Diana asked, shivering.

"It'll warm up," John said confidently, "but if it doesn't, we can ride in the arena. Besides, you want to see Galaxy and the foal, don't you?"

"I do," she admitted, surrendering to his suggestions. "And right now, I want to eat my lunch."

"With me." It wasn't a question. When they returned to the lunchroom, she had to force herself not to look toward the table where she could hear Jeremy laughing with the others.

To Diana's surprise, the weather followed John's prediction and they had a perfect afternoon for riding. She had trouble concentrating on John's conversation about football and wrestling and all the other things he was interested in. Her mind kept returning to those moments when Jeremy had faced John and argued for her. It sent shivers up her spine to think that he'd been defending her. And he seemed to understand her need to make her own decisions, unlike John.

"Hey, come back to earth, Diana," John said, interrupting her thoughts. "What about tomorrow night?"

"Tomorrow night?" She swallowed guiltily.

"Would you like to do something?" John looked impatient. "We could go dancing or maybe see another movie, whatever you'd like to do."

"That's sweet of you, John," Diana began, regretting her earlier cowardice. She should have told John about her date with Jeremy before. "I'd love to go out with you, but I have other plans."

"What kind of other plans?"

"Bart and I were invited to a party Phoebe Hall is giving," Diana answered. It wasn't the whole truth, but it was close enough that it wasn't really a lie, either.

"Do you have to go?"

"I don't have to, John, I *want* to."

"You're going with that Jeremy Stone, aren't you?" His tone and gaze were filled with hurt and accusation.

Diana nodded. "He asked me Sunday."

John glared at her, then reined his horse around and galloped back toward the stable. Diana's mount leaped forward in pursuit, but she held him back. At the moment she didn't really want to talk to John. He was too angry and she needed some time to think. He really was beginning to be overbearing and she wasn't quite sure how to handle it. And she couldn't deny the way the thought of being with Jeremy made her feel.

Though she rode back slowly, and thought about the two boys the entire time, she was no closer to knowing what to say or do when she reached the stable, than she had been when John asked her out. She found him waiting at the stableyard gate.

"Are you still going on the hayride with me?" he demanded.

"I want to," she answered, "if you want me to."

"I want you to be my girlfriend," John said quietly. "I've never felt this way about anyone before, Diana."

Diana caught her breath, stunned by the words and by the look on John's face. For a moment her head swirled with excitement, then another face filled her thoughts — Jeremy's. The thrill faded.

"Don't you want that, too, Diana?" he asked.

"I'm very flattered, John, and I like you a lot, but I just moved here. I'm not ready to make a commitment yet." She dismounted and allowed him to take her horse into the stable, then lead her to the car. Once in the car, he put his arm around her and kissed her very gently, first on the cheek, then lightly on the lips.

"I want you to think about it," he said. "We can talk about it on the hayride Saturday night. By then maybe you'll be ready to make a commitment."

Diana smiled at him, still too confused about her own feelings to say anything more. John, however, didn't seem to notice her silence as he drove her back to Rose Hill. He chatted away about the wrestling championship he'd won last year and his plans for investigating the wrestling programs at the various colleges he might want to attend next year. He, at least, seemed to have no doubt about what her reply would be.

Diana found it hard to concentrate on her homework after dinner. Two faces kept coming between her and the pages — John's all full of entreaty, Jeremy's glowing with excitement at the prospect of the video project. What in the world was she going to do? she asked herself. How could she choose?

Friday morning when she got to school, she found Jeremy waiting for her at her desk in homeroom.

"I'm sorry about yesterday," he began. "I didn't realize that Marquette was so touchy. I guess I shouldn't have said anything, but. . . ." He stopped to take a breath. "You are still going to the party with me tonight, aren't you?"

"Of course," Diana said, her smile easing his fears. "And it was my fault, too. I hadn't mentioned the video to John and I hadn't told him about the party, either."

"He doesn't own you, Diana," Jeremy said, angry at the way she seemed to be deferring to John. "I really wish you would eat lunch with us sometimes. I hardly ever get to see you." He stood there silently for a moment, hoping she would say something, tell him that she wanted to join them as much as he wanted her to, but she said nothing.

"I was planning to leave for the party at about five," he continued. "Is that all right with you? I don't want to rush you or anything."

"I'll be ready," she promised.

Their eyes locked for a brief second and she felt that same tingling excitement she'd felt Sunday when he held her hand. The sound of the bell forced him to return to his own desk and Diana reprimanded herself for not letting him know how much she liked him. Well, they still had the long drive to the Halls' cabin and she could hardly wait for five o'clock to come.

By four o'clock, Diana was overcome with excitement and anticipation. Phoebe and Sasha had assured her it was a very casual party, so she'd settled on blue jeans, an oversized blue and white checked shirt and her cowboy boots. She decided to wear her hair down, and she brushed the soft blonde waves over and over again as she waited nervously for Jeremy to arrive.

Chapter 7

The long drive passed swiftly and Diana was already enjoying herself tremendously. Jeremy was full of stories about life in England and some of the other places he'd lived when his father was assigned to different foreign embassies. He had dozens of questions about her life, too, and he didn't bring up taking her picture even once. It was incredibly easy to talk to him, and she was feeling relaxed and content when they finally arrived.

The cabin was a shock. It was located in a remote area in the mountains and didn't even have a phone or electricity. Light came from kerosene lamps and the decor was definitely rustic. Outside there were two grills set up and Phoebe and Woody were busy stirring the coals, preparing to cook stacks of hamburgers and hot dogs.

"Come on, I'll put you to work, Diana,"

Phoebe called. "Bart and Ted are setting up the picnic tables, so you can start carrying stuff out."

"Hi, Diana. How have you been? I haven't seen you all week," Sasha said, coming up beside her. "Why haven't you been eating lunch with us?"

"Well, John has been keeping me pretty busy," Diana answered.

"Don't let him isolate you from us, Diana," Phoebe advised, joining them. "Friends are important and there are a lot of other people for you to get to know."

"Oh, Phoebe, Sasha, I'm so confused. I'd love to eat lunch with the rest of you guys, but John has become sort of possessive and I don't really know what to tell him."

"There are a lot of school activities, Diana," Sasha said. "It would be fun to have you join us for some of them."

"I . . . I don't know what to say," Diana murmured, picking up a load of dishes and carrying them out to the picnic tables. She knew they were right. She was definitely isolating herself by spending so much time with John. She wanted to be friends with Phoebe and Sasha, to be a part of the crowd. But she also wouldn't mind having a boyfriend. John obviously wasn't part of their group, and Jeremy hadn't exactly asked her to go steady the way John had.

She looked around for Bart, longing for the company of someone familiar. She wanted to know what he thought of her dilemma. Maybe he could help her straighten things out, figure out how to stay a part of the crowd while still spending time with John.

"Maybe he wants Diana to be in it," Bart suggested, enjoying the tension he sensed between the two girls. "He keeps telling her he wants to take her picture. But anyway, tell me what everybody does at these parties," Bart said with a lazy grin. "I mean after we eat all that food."

"We build a bonfire and sing or tell ghost stories," Chris said, coming back to join them. "The food is officially ready for serving according to Phoebe, but there's still as much left in the kitchen as we have on the tables."

"My kind of party," Bart said, leading the way to the food. "Let's go see how much of it we can make disappear."

Gloria gritted her teeth and moved with the trio. They weren't going to cut her out, she vowed. Bart was always flirting with everyone — even quiet Janie Barstow. Gloria didn't care so much about winning Bart, but more than anything she wanted to be part of the crowd. She had to keep his interest at least until she was accepted.

Jeremy watched Diana setting food on the table.

She looked troubled and he walked up to her and took her hand. "Diana, are you all right?" he asked.

She turned and smiled halfheartedly. "Sure, Jeremy," she said. "What's up?"

"Are you about ready to eat?" he asked. "I'm starving." He couldn't believe the things that came out of his mouth when all he wanted was to let

Diana know what he thought of her. "Aren't you hungry?"

"Definitely," she smiled. He squeeezed her hand and said, "Come on, let's give our orders to Ted. Phoebe says he grills a mean hamburger. After that, you'll have to teach me all the secrets of survival at a picnic like this. I assume you're used to cookouts at the ranch."

Diana laughed. "Well, we get to eat inside once in a while. I don't think I've ever seen so much food," she said, looking at the spread.

"Good, I want you to eat until you're too full to argue with me," Jeremy teased. "Then we're going to talk some more about the fashion video."

"Fashion video?" Diana felt her uneasiness slipping away as Jeremy talked. "When was that decided?"

"At lunch today. It was Janie's idea. It will be like a fashion show of Henry's designs, but on video."

"That's a great idea," Diana said. "I've seen some of the clothes he's made for Janie and I love them. I'm already saving up my money to buy a dress from him."

"Anyway, getting back to the video, I still want to take pictures of you," Jeremy reminded her.

"Tell me about the video class," Diana said, "and about the fashion video."

He began to talk about the video class and soon he and Diana were deep in conversation. Everyone else at the picnic seemed to fade into the background as Jeremy kept Diana captivated. She had a strange and unfamiliar feeling in the pit of her stomach that intensified every time Jeremy looked deep into her eyes or brushed his hand against hers. She suddenly began to wonder if she was falling in love with him.

After everyone had eaten their fill, Bart got to his feet and went to the station wagon. "Since this is an old-fashioned picnic," Bart said, "I thought maybe I could pay for my supper the way I did at picnics back home. If you'll all help me out." He held up a battered old guitar. "Sing-along?"

Gloria watched as Brenda and Sasha crowded around him, all chattering at once. There was no room for her near him now, that was plain. She looked around the crowd and her eyes came to rest on Diana and Jeremy.

She walked over to them and sat down beside Jeremy. She seemed uninterested in Bart's playing and instead of listening she began to ask Jeremy questions about the video. Diana noticed and felt a twinge of jealousy, but she kept on singing as Jeremy and Gloria talked.

"You know," Gloria said, "it's too bad the hayride is so soon. That could make an interesting background for your video screening, don't you think?"

He grinned. "I suppose it could be, but I'm glad it's just for fun. I've never been on one and I just want to relax and enjoy it, not think about schoolwork."

"Are you going?" Diana overheard, and broke into the conversation. She was surprised by the mixture of emotions she felt at the idea. She wanted to spend more time with Jeremy, but knew she was committed to going on the hayride with John. After what had happened in the lunchroom yesterday, she hated to think of what might happen on the hayride. What a mess everything was becoming.

"Yeah, we're all going," Jeremy answered. "I can't wait. Do we really ride in a wagon full of hay with horses pulling it, or do they use trucks nowadays?"

"I don't know for sure," Diana admitted. "But since we'll be at the stable, I'd think real horses."

"You're going with John, aren't you, Diana?" Gloria asked, smiling sweetly.

Diana nodded. "His sister owns the stable that's sponsoring it," she said, uncomfortable at the mention of John's name.

Gloria turned to Jeremy. "Do you think I could catch a ride with you, Jeremy? I don't have any idea where the stable is."

Jeremy laughed. "I don't, either," he said. "I'm going with Woody and Kim. I'm sure you can ride along with us."

"But what about Bart?" Diana blurted out.

"He's not going," Gloria said. "He says he's been on enough hayrides to last him a lifetime."

"I bet he'll be sorry he missed it when we tell him all the fun we had," Jeremy said.

Diana was furious with Gloria, and she definitely felt a pang of jealousy as Gloria smiled up at Jeremy. She felt more confused than ever. She had a date with John for the hayride, so why should she care if Gloria went with Jeremy? But suddenly she wished she were going with Jeremy instead of John. She was glad when Gloria finally went to join the girls who were crowded around Bart, leaving her alone with Jeremy. She edged over closer to him and rested her head against his shoulder, shivering when he placed his arm around her and pulled her even closer. They stayed like that until it was time to go home.

Too soon Jeremy was stopping his car in front of Diana's house and she felt surprisingly reluctant to leave him. They both got out of the car and he walked her to the door. She felt her heartbeat quicken as he took her hand and said, "I'm really glad you came with me tonight, Diana. I'd love it if you'd go out with me again soon."

"I'd like to," she whispered, digging her key out of her pocket. "I had a fantastic time tonight."

They stood together, staring at each other, then Jeremy boldly leaned over and brushed her lips with his. It was a soft, quick kiss — but she was ecstatic. "See you tomorrow at the hayride," he called, walking back to his car.

"Good-night," Diana said, her pleasure quickly fading. She suddenly found herself wishing for rain tomorrow — anything to postpone another confrontation between Jeremy and John.

Chapter
8

Saturday dawned sunny and beautiful, a perfect day for a hayride. "You should be going with us tonight," Diana told Bart as they sat in the kitchen eating lunch. "It's going to be fun."

Bart shrugged. "I've been on plenty of hayrides in my lifetime."

"Gloria was pretty disappointed, I think," Diana continued. "She's going, you know."

"So how did you and the mad movie maker get along?" Bart asked, obviously not wanting to talk about Gloria.

"I really like him," Diana said. "We had a great time last night."

"So where does that leave good old John?"

"He's nice, too." Diana stared at her sandwich, then confided, "John asked me to go out with him, Bart. What do you think I should do?"

"Do you want to?"

"Not really. I like him and we've been having

fun together, but I don't want to be confined to seeing just him. I want to go out with other boys, too."

"Like Jeremy?" Bart asked, grinning at her. "Just tell John that, Diana. He may not like it, but I think you should be honest with him. He's pretty crazy about you."

"I don't want to hurt his feelings, Bart. I think he's really counting on me to say I'll go with him."

Bart laughed. "According to the guys on the football team, you'd need a sledgehammer to hurt his feelings. He's really got a bad reputation — I mean, he's a good player, but he's got a mean temper."

"That's so hard to believe," Diana protested. "He's been so sweet and considerate to me." Then she remembered his outburst of anger in the lunchroom.

"Well, it has to be your decision, Diana," Bart told her. "You have to decide how you feel — that's what's important."

Diana nodded, knowing he was right; the problem was, she wasn't sure how she felt. It was all too new and exciting and she didn't want to do the wrong thing and hurt anyone.

John's flowers were delivered about one in the afternoon and she felt a pang of guilt as she sniffed the sweet fragrance of the pale pink roses. He was sweet, no matter what other people thought, and he did care about her a lot. She still hadn't decided what she would tell him later that night when he showed up promptly at five-thirty.

"You'd better bring a warm jacket," he advised after accepting her thanks for the roses and complimenting her on how pretty she looked. "It gets cold in the hills after the sun goes down."

"Is that where we're going?" Diana asked, obediently getting a sturdy leather jacket from the hall closet.

"It's the only place we can go with horses and wagons," John said. "They'd tie up traffic for miles if we tried to go out on the highway. There's a country road we can follow and a nice spot for the cookout on the shore of a pond. It should be real romantic." His voice softened and he touched her hand. "So, are you ready to go?"

Diana nodded, her stomach knotted with indecision. She liked John so much and she remembered vividly the magical moment they'd shared the first afternoon they had spent together. How could she reject him? Then she thought of Jeremy and the promise of that feathery kiss. She didn't want to give that up, either.

Danberry Stable was a beehive of activity when they arrived. Five big farm wagons loaded with loose straw were being readied for the carloads of people who were coming. Diana gasped. "I had no idea there would be so many people," she said.

John laughed. "When Irene does something for charity, she does it right. 'Horses for the Handicapped' is her pet project and she figures this one hayride will keep two or three horses in oats and hay for a year."

"Here?" Diana asked.

He nodded. "She has classes three or four times a week for blind and handicapped kids and adults. It's hard to find horses that are gentle enough to work with the handicapped and this is publicity for the cause that raises money, too."

A chorus of greetings ended the conversation and Diana turned to welcome Jeremy, Gloria, Woody, Kim, Peter, and Monica. A moment later a second car discharged Phoebe, Michael, and Sasha.

"What did you do, tell everyone at school?" John asked Diana, as he glared at Jeremy.

"Everybody thought it would be fun," Diana said. "And it's good for your sister's project, anyway. The more people, the more money she can raise."

John started to say something, then was called away by his brother-in-law. Jeremy walked over to Diana. "Your date doesn't seem to be too happy to see us," he said.

"I think he wanted to be alone with Diana," Gloria said, putting a hand on Jeremy's arm. "It's no secret that he's crazy about her."

Diana wished Gloria away, but kept her smile in place. "I'm glad all of you decided to come," she said, trying to tell Jeremy with a glance that the words were truly meant for him.

"You couldn't have kept me away," Jeremy replied, and for a moment their eyes locked and she was sure he was feeling the same wild emotions that she was.

"Come on, Diana," John said, shattering the

moment as he took her arm. "Irene wants us to ride in the lead wagon so we can help arrange things at the other end. She and Jack can't handle everything with a crowd this large." He half-dragged her away from Jeremy.

"What about the rest of the kids?" Diana asked, looking back at her friends. "Can't they ride in the first wagon, too?"

"There isn't enough room," John said, picking her up and setting her on the end of the wagon, then vaulting up beside her. "You'll see them at the pond."

Diana sighed, then waved to the others as the wagon lurched forward. She sensed that John's bad manners came from jealousy, but that didn't make her feel any better. It was not a particularly promising beginning for the evening, and she had a horrible feeling it was going to get worse instead of better.

John's mood changed immediately and her fears faded slightly as they rode through the gorgeous countryside. Diana soon found herself describing Montana hayrides and some of her adventures on the ranch to Jack and Irene.

At the cookout, she was so busy she hardly had time to talk to John. She'd volunteered to help Irene with the serving and Jack had asked John to work at the big grill, helping him with the steaks, so they could only smile in passing until all the food was served. When they got their own loaded plates, John led her to the area where Jack and Irene were sitting.

"You should go eat with your friends from

school," Irene said as they sat down on the ground. "You two have done enough. You were supposed to be guests."

"Diana wanted to ask you about your classes for the handicapped," John said, looking pleased with himself.

"That's true," Diana admitted. She was looking across the campfire to where Gloria was sitting curled up next to Jeremy. They certainly look like they're having a good time, she thought unhappily. She forced herself to push thoughts of Jeremy out of her mind and concentrate on Irene. Her first question opened a conversation that kept her busy through the rest of the meal. She was surprised when Jack got up and said, "Time for me to get back to work."

"And time for us to take a little walk," John said, eyeing her warmly.

"Shouldn't we stay here and join in the singing?" Diana asked, knowing at once that John intended to pressure her into a commitment again.

"Don't you want to be alone with me, Diana?" John asked, sounding hurt. "Did something happen at that party last night?"

Diana looked around, aware that John's voice was rising and that the people nearby were staring at them. "Nothing happened," she said. "Please, John, I just thought. . . ."

"Come on," he said, slipping his arm around her shoulders. "We have something to talk about, Diana."

His arm was too strong for her to pull away, so

there was nothing to do but leave the moonlit clearing and step into the deep shadow of trees that ringed the pond. She stumbled along beside him, feeling miserable. Finally she dug in her heels. "This is far enough, John," she said.

They stopped walking, but he didn't let her go. Instead he pulled her close and began to kiss her. She found herself wondering what it would be like to kiss Jeremy, and she quickly broke away.

"John, please don't." She tried to pull away out of his grasp, but he held her tightly.

"I'm sorry, Diana," he groaned. "It's just that I'm so crazy about you. When I see you with Stone and the rest of his crowd, I go kind of nuts."

"John, I like you a lot," Diana began, hating the guilt that spread through her, "but I really don't want to get serious yet. I want to have the chance to get to know you and everyone else better."

His arms tightened like steel bands around her. "Oh, Diana, how can you say no? We can have so much together. It's special for us. Please don't say no."

She felt a chill of fear, not of John, but of the intensity of his feelings for her. "It's too soon, John," she murmured. "You have to give me some time. You scare me when you act like this."

His embrace loosened at once. "I didn't mean to scare you," he said. "You're my girl, Diana, I'd never hurt you. Please don't be angry."

"I'm not," Diana assured him. "I just don't want to talk about getting more serious. Not yet. I just want to enjoy myself and get used to my new life in Rose Hill. Will you give me the chance, John?"

His fingers touched her cheek and she sensed the love in his caress. "You know I'll give you anything you want," he said. "Just promise that you'll keep thinking about making it official."

"I promise to keep thinking about it," Diana said, but when his lips touched hers again, her thoughts were on Jeremy, and she felt tears burning in her eyes. This wasn't the way it was supposed to be — falling in love was supposed to be wonderful, and it was supposed to happen to two people at the same time. "Could we go back to the fire now?" she asked when he let her go.

"Whatever you want, Diana," he said and his sad tone made her feel even worse. "Just forgive me for scaring you, okay? I don't like it when you're mad at me."

"Let's just forget the whole thing," Diana suggested. "We were having such a nice time with Irene and Jack, I'd like to go back to that."

"Right." His voice told her that he wasn't happy, but the rest of the evening passed without incident and he even managed to be cordial to Jeremy.

The evening never improved for Diana, though. Every time she looked around for Jeremy, she saw him listening intently to Gloria or laughing with her. And Gloria certainly didn't seem to be missing Bart, Diana noticed. In fact, she seemed perfectly happy with Jeremy.

John was true to his word, not pressing her for more than a brief kiss as they rode back on the last wagon with the Kennedy High crowd. He didn't even mention their earlier conversation when he drove her home. All he said when he walked her to the door was, "Just remember that I love you, Diana, and I'm going to make you love me." He kissed her quickly and left before she could say a word.

Chapter 9

By the time she sat down at the table for Sunday dinner, Diana was beginning to think she'd made a mistake refusing John. He'd called twice to talk and to apologize again for frightening her. A second bouquet of roses was filling the air of the dining room, rivaling the rich aroma of pot roast and apple pie, her father's favorite meal.

Bart grinned at her as they began to eat. "Do those mean that you said yes?" he asked, pointing to the flowers.

"Yes to what?" her mother inquired.

"Going with John," Diana answered. "And no it doesn't. I told him that I wasn't ready."

"Good for you, Diana," her mother said.

"So why the roses?" Bart asked.

"Because I'm irresistible," Diana told him, giggling.

"What you are is . . ." he began, then stopped as the phone rang. He and Diana both started to get up, but their father was already on his feet.

"I'll get it," he said, heading for the study.

"Who was that, dear?" Rose asked when he finally came back to the dining room.

Donald Einerson sighed. "That was Claxton," he said. "I have to go to the office for an emergency meeting."

"Today?"

"I told him I'd be there in about an hour."

"Donald, you promised me that you'd stay home with us today. We never see you. This is the first real meal you've had with all of us since the children arrived."

"Honey, I didn't plan this," he said between bites. "I don't want to go, but that's the way it is in politics. This is a crisis situation and I have to be there."

For a moment Diana thought her mother was going to object further, but she closed her mouth without speaking. Diana watched her, conscious of her mother's hurt feelings. They ate quickly and in almost total silence. It was a relief when her father rose.

"I'm sorry, Rose," he said, "but it really is an important meeting. I'll be home just as soon as I can."

Bart finished his second piece of pie, then got up, too. "I think I'll go for a walk, maybe stop by the sub shop," he said, then looked at Diana. "You want to come along?"

Diana started to nod, then glanced at her mother and changed her mind. "I don't think so," she said. "I'll help Mom with the dishes."

Her mother said nothing, just sat staring at

the empty chair at the head of the table, her expression unreadable. Finally, she turned to Diana, and said, "Go with Bart, Diana. I don't need any help with the dishes and it doesn't look like it's going to be family day at the Einerson house after all."

Diana hesitated, but her mother's expression didn't change and she realized that there wasn't anything she could do. She ran outside and shouted at Bart to wait for her.

Gloria smiled at Jeremy as she huddled close to him in his darkroom. "These are wonderful," she said. "I'm so glad you let me see some of your work."

"Well, I don't mind showing my photos to anyone who's so interested in photography," Jeremy said, feeling a little foolish. He hadn't invited Gloria over to see his photographs, but when she'd come to the door, he couldn't just turn her away.

"Will you teach me how to take pictures like these?" Gloria asked, looking up at him with flattering adoration. "I mean, I know I won't be as good as you are, but I see so many things that I'd like to photograph and then my pictures come out so ordinary."

"Well, sure," Jeremy said, "sometime soon. For a while I think I'm going to be kind of busy planning the video."

"I'd really like to help you with it. Don't you need an assistant?" Gloria pressed. "I mean, I'm not taking the class, but I'd be willing to do whatever you want. I could take notes on all the plans and carry equipment and keep things organized and. . . ." She stopped, looking down as though too shy to go on. "That is, if you need an assistant," she said softly.

"That's a great idea," Jeremy said with more enthusiasm than he felt. "We can use someone to keep things straight. Every time we start planning, everybody talks at once and we have so many ideas, we can't settle on anything."

"I'll start this afternoon," Gloria said with a smile that positively glowed. "Isn't everyone meeting at the sub shop later today?"

Jeremy nodded, suddenly regretting his acceptance of her offer. What if Diana was there? He'd seen the way she looked at him last night when Gloria snuggled up beside him. But then, she'd been with Marquette last night. He cursed himself for not having asked for another date when they were out Friday night.

"Shouldn't we get going?" Gloria asked with a seductive smile.

Jeremy took a deep breath. "Yeah, it is getting pretty late," he said, feeling trapped. Gloria was making him uncomfortable. All he could think about was Diana, remembering the gentle pressure of her head against his shoulder, the fresh scent of her hair, the sweetness of her lips when he'd kissed her.

He forced the images from his mind and headed for the sub shop with Gloria. It wasn't until they were inside and halfway across the room that he realized Diana was there. He was delighted, until he saw Diana look up and then quickly away. She thought he was with Gloria, he realized.

It was agony sitting down at the table trying to concentrate on the conversation about the video when all he wanted to do was talk to Diana alone, but there was nothing he could do. Gloria insisted on babbling about his photographs and making it sound like he had invited her over. Diana sat there silently, avoiding his eyes, bending and unbending a straw. She and Bart left early, and Jeremy never had a chance to say a word to her.

He sat there daydreaming about Diana until he overheard Gloria talking about John Marquette.

"John was going to ask her to go with him at the hayride last night," she was saying.

"How do you know that?" Jeremy demanded, not caring that the others were watching him.

"John told me at school on Friday," Gloria answered. "That's why I was so surprised to see you with Diana that night, Jeremy. He seemed so sure that she'd accept. I mean, he's crazy about her and she seems to like him a lot." She giggled. "I saw them wandering off into the woods after dinner."

Jeremy said nothing, not wanting to believe her. He just couldn't picture Diana with that burly wrestler. He was all wrong for her. He got to his feet.

"You leaving?" Woody asked.

"Yeah, I've got some things to do," Jeremy said, scarcely looking back as he started for the door. "See you guys tomorrow."

"He's acting weird," Sasha noted.

"I think he has Diana fever," Chris said. "Are you sure about Diana and John, Gloria? I got the feeling she really liked Jeremy when they were at the party Friday."

Gloria shrugged, then opened her notebook. "I really don't know the details of Diana's love life, but I do think we should talk some more about the video," she said. "We haven't even decided what sort of clothes we're going to use."

When she got home, Diana went straight to her room, muttering about doing her homework. But when she sat down and opened her math book, she found that she couldn't focus on anything. She kept seeing Jeremy walking into the sub shop with Gloria. They'd spent the whole evening together on the hayride and now he was showing her his photographs.

Was she crazy? she asked herself. John was clearly in love with her, while Jeremy hadn't shown much interest in her at all. She had no idea how *he* felt about *her* and *she* couldn't get *him* out of her mind. He hadn't even tried to talk to her at the sub shop today. Had he forgotten what a great time they'd had at the mountain cabin already, now that Gloria was in the picture? Diana felt like screaming and throwing things as she paced around her room before collapsing on the bed in tears.

The next morning she resolved to get to homeroom early to talk to Jeremy and find out if he was serious about Gloria. She had to know where things stood with him. To her surprise, he was waiting at her desk when she arrived.

"I was hoping you'd be early," he said, looking shy and uncomfortable.

"And I was hoping you would be," Diana murmured, almost tongue-tied now that she was facing him.

"I wanted to ask you to eat lunch with the rest of us today. I want to talk to you about the past couple of days," he said softly, staring at his feet. "And we're also going to talk about who's going to be in the video."

"Do you still want me to be in it?"

"Of course I do. And so does everyone else. I'd still like to take some photographs of you, too, Diana. That way you could see what the camera is going to capture when we actually get to the taping of the video."

The idea of posing for Jeremy sent currents of excitement through her, but before she could say anything John's large frame moved in between her and Jeremy.

"Hi, gorgeous," he said, draping his arm casually around her shoulders. "I missed you yesterday, so I thought maybe this would let you know how much." He handed her a small box, then gave her a light kiss on the cheek. "Aren't you going to open it?" he asked, when she hesitated.

He was looking at her so pleadingly, she could feel the red rising in her cheeks. She was aware of the sudden cooling in Jeremy's expression. "You're very sweet," she murmured, fumbling with the box lid as she tried to make her fingers

91

work. When she finally opened the box, she found a tiny silver charm in the shape of a horse nestled on a bed of tissue.

"I wanted you to remember Saturday night," John said. "A special time deserves a special present, right?"

Tears welled up in her eyes and she had to blink hard to keep them back. "It's . . . it's lovely," she managed. "Thank you so much, John." The first bell rang, echoing loudly in the now-silent room.

"See you later," John said, giving her shoulders a gentle squeeze, then heading for the door.

Diana just stood there, looking down at the miniature horse, her mind filled with memories of Saturday night — most of them more painful than special. By the time she looked up, seeking Jeremy, he was across the room in his own seat. He was staring straight ahead so she couldn't see his expression, but the stiffness of his shoulders seemed like an accusation and again she felt the tears behind her eyes. She still hadn't had a chance to get things straight with Jeremy. Why wouldn't John leave her alone? The second bell rang and Diana put the cover back on the box, shutting out the memories.

Her morning classes passed quickly but all she could think of was how to let Jeremy know he was important to her. She hoped it wasn't too late. Her mind was still on Jeremy as she stepped out into the busy corridor and headed for her locker to pick up her lunch.

"Hi, Diana, ready for lunch?" John was leaning on the wall, his smile broad, a little less confident than usual. "I brought some of my Mom's special brownies."

She gulped, feeling overwhelmed by guilt. "I promised to have lunch with Jeremy and Henry and Woody to discuss the fashion video," she said, speaking quickly, trying to get the words out before she lost her nerve.

"You're still planning to be in that thing?" John asked. "It's just a dumb class project, and you're not even in the class."

"I promised, John," Diana said. "You can eat with us, too, you know."

She had a few more things to say, but his glare was so furious the words froze in her throat. It seemed their eyes locked for hours before he turned and stomped away down the hall. Diana sagged against the wall to catch her breath, then let it out in a sigh of relief before hurrying to her locker to drop off her books and get her lunch. She was having lunch with Jeremy and she'd manage to let him know that it was not only because he'd asked her to, but because she wanted to.

She felt a little shy approaching the benches under the cherry trees on the quad where everyone was gathered in the fall sunshine. Janie looked up, waved, then patted the bench beside her. "Come look at this," she said. "It's Henry's sketch of the dress he wants you to wear in the video."

Diana sat down beside her and looked at the sketch. Immediately all her worries were forgotten. "Oh, Henry, it's gorgeous."

"You like it?" He looked pleased.

"Like it? It's the most beautiful dress I've ever

seen. But are you sure it's my style? I'm the jeans and cowboy boots type — remember?"

"That's not true," Jeremy said. "That dress is perfect for you. Color, line, everything will be right."

Diana blushed at the praise, and touched the tiny swatch of silky fabric clipped to the top. The aquamarine gown was asymmetrical, with gathers to enhance her figure, a fan of pleats to create a focal point on the shoulder, a seam to draw the eye to the high slit in the narrow skirt. She ached to try it on.

"If you don't want to wear it, I'd love to," Laurie said.

"So would I," Brenda agreed.

"Well, I like the one Henry's picked for me," Chris said, holding up the sketch she'd been looking at.

The black evening gown was cut high in front. Two bands encrusted with beads rose from the hem, curved in at the waistline, then out and up to the shoulders. The back was a pencil-thin X of black fabric that secured the gown across the shoulder blades.

"How do you have the time to do all these?" Diana asked Henry.

"They're already done," Henry said. "One of the shops in Georgetown asked me to do a line of evening gowns for their holiday display and we worked on them this summer. We just have to shoot the video before the end of October, because they have to be delivered by November first."

"We'll do it," Jeremy promised, "right, assistant?" He turned to Gloria with smile that took all the joy out of Diana.

The conversation went on, but Diana couldn't pay attention to anything. All she could think of was Jeremy and Gloria as a couple. She kept imagining Gloria in Jeremy's arms, kissing him, so she was relieved when Sasha said, "We'd better get going. It's time for class."

Before Diana could leave the bench, Jeremy caught her hand. "You will come round tomorrow for lunch, won't you?" he asked, his blue-gray eyes boring into her. The intensity of his gaze made her shiver.

She found herself nodding as all the magic of the night she'd spent with him came flooding back — until Gloria came over and pulled Jeremy away, mumbling about the math quiz they had next period.

Diana ran to her locker, glad that the halls were nearly empty so no one could see her tears.

Chapter
10

When she got to her locker, John was standing there waiting. His warm smile simply made
her feel worse. "Have a nice lunch?" he asked
sarcastically.

"I don't even remember eating," she admitted.
"You should see the dress Henry wants me to
wear. It's incredible, John. I can't wait to try it
on."

His smile vanished. "You're really going to do
it, aren't you?" he asked. "You don't even care
how I feel about it. Or maybe you prefer having
lunch with that bunch to being with me."

"It's not that, John," Diana protested, even
though she had a feeling he was right. "Besides
the fact that I like them, we're using the time to
make plans for the video. I don't know why you
won't eat with us. Not everyone there is involved
with the video."

John snorted. "I'd rather eat with the team. Tell

old Bart when he gets tired of making eyes at all the girls in that crowd, he can join the big boys and stop playing with the wimps."

"Oh, John, really . . ." she began, but he'd already turned and disappeared around the corner. Sighing, she opened her locker and took out her books. She barely made it to class before the final bell.

The next few days passed in similar fashion. John was forever lurking here and there in the corridors, glaring or looking sad-eyed at her from a distance. He didn't ask her to eat lunch with him again and because he had football practice after school every day, he couldn't drive her home. She couldn't really say she missed his company.

Instead she spent her free time with the group, stopping by the sub shop nearly every afternoon and joining in the discussion about the fashion video. It was getting harder and harder to get Jeremy out of her thoughts, and spending time with him was becoming increasingly frustrating. No matter how she smiled at him or tried to strike up a conversation, he was cool and distant. She never had a moment alone with him, and he certainly didn't seem to be making the effort to talk to her alone. It was as though he had absolutely no interest in her, and it was driving her crazy.

Then on Thursday, John was waiting for her outside her homeroom when she arrived at school. "I'd like to take you out tomorrow night," he said. "I know you don't have time to see me at lunch anymore, but we could have dinner and go out dancing, if you'd like to." He hesitated, as

97

though expecting her to answer. When she didn't, he continued. "Please, Diana, I really missed you a lot this week. I want to spend some time with you."

Her guilt returned and with it a longing for the uncomplicated ease she'd felt with John the first time they'd gone out. She'd hoped each noon and each afternoon that Jeremy would ask her out, but he hadn't so much as held her hand since Phoebe's party.

"We could go riding Saturday, too," John continued. "And there's a new movie in town that sounds good. Please say you'll go out with me, Diana, I don't care where we go or what we do. I just want to be with you."

She forced thoughts of Jeremy out of her head. "I'd love to go out with you, John," she began, telling herself that it was the truth, feeling that it was not. Dating John was the best way to banish the hurt Jeremy's treatment was causing her. It would be good for her to spend some time with someone who really cared about her.

John hugged her happily, practically lifting her off the floor in his joy. When he set her back on her feet, his grin was so wide she almost laughed. But all of a sudden she realized she was taking advantage of John's feelings for her.

What in the world was she doing? What if she hurt John the way Jeremy was hurting her? Well, it was too late to back out now. She'd have to try to explain to John tomorrow night that she didn't feel the same way he did. She wanted to be friends — she did like him — but she knew now that she could never return the feelings he was offering and it was unfair to lead him on.

"Six-thirty tomorrow night," John said. "We'll have dinner somewhere nice, then decide what to do with the rest of the evening."

"Great," Diana said, furious with herself, but unable to say anything else. Swallowing a sigh, she entered the classroom and sank down behind her desk. Nothing seemed to be working out the way she wanted it to. She glanced over at Jeremy, who didn't look her way once. She still couldn't believe he had entirely forgotten the magic moments they'd shared the night of Phoebe's party.

She was surprised when Jeremy stopped by her locker after lunch.

"Will you be at the sub shop after school?" he asked.

Her dark eyes were troubled as she looked up at him. "Not today," she said.

"Oh, going out with John?" He tried to keep the bitterness out of his voice, but from the hurt look on her face, he knew he hadn't succeeded.

"No, I've decided to go riding alone," Diana said. "I've got some decisions to make and I can think clearly on a horse."

"Jeremy, come on. . . ." Gloria appeared out of nowhere, and Jeremy turned to follow her to class.

Jeremy quickly threw several canisters of extra film into his camera bag and zipped it shut. He knew he couldn't waste any more time. Diana had said she was going to make a decision, and if it had anything to do with the way he'd been acting for the past few days, it could only be a decision that would make him even more miserable than he already was. So he had to go look for Diana at Danberry Stable. He was afraid she had decided not to be in the video, and he wanted one last chance to convince her otherwise. Besides, it was really time to straighten things out, let her know how much he liked her. He got his bike from the garage and pedaled fast toward Danberry Stable.

Her bike was parked near one of the white stable buildings, but as he placed his beside it, he realized that he had no idea where she might have gone once she got here. He looked around, not sure what to do next.

"Can I help you?" Irene Danberry asked, then smiled as she recognized him from the night of the hayride.

"I was looking for Diana Einerson," he said. "Do you know where I could find her?"

"I think she was riding out toward the pond where we had the cookout," Irene said. "Did you want to rent a horse?"

Jeremy shook his head. "Not if I can get there on my bike," he admitted. "I'd love to learn to ride sometime, but today I really have to talk to Diana."

"Well, if she's at the pond, you can follow the same road we used for the haywagons," Irene told him. "That one over there," she pointed.

"Thank you," he said, getting on his bike again and pedaling strongly away from the buildings.

The pond area looked different in daylight than it had the night of the hayride, but Jeremy didn't really appreciate the beauty of the setting until he saw the bay horse tied to a tree. One horse — she was alone. He left his bike against a tree and made his way toward the pond. Diana was sitting on a log near where the campfire had been. She didn't look up until a dry stick crunched beneath his feet.

"Jeremy!" she gasped, jumping up. "What are you doing here?"

"Looking for you." The words were out before he thought.

"Why?"

He didn't know what to say. He suddenly felt foolish for thinking she might be dropping out of the video, so he held up his camera. "To take your picture," he said, already feeling more confident. "I keep asking you and you're always too busy or something, so I thought maybe you wouldn't mind if I came out here to do it."

"But I must look awful," she said, running her hand through hair that had grown wild from her ride.

"Shh," Jeremy said, placing a finger lightly on her lips. "Will you trust me? Please."

For a moment he thought that she might refuse, then suddenly her expression changed, and her eyes began to shine the way they had when he'd first seen her. "If you don't think I'll break your camera, go ahead," she said, laughing. "What do you want me to do?"

Jeremy suddenly took control and Diana saw a side of him she'd never seen before — he was firm, demanding, totally in command. He told her where and how to stand, made her turn slightly, move her head, her hands, her entire body in new ways. He rearranged her hair, asked her to project a variety of emotions, all without giving her a chance to object.

"I think that's enough," Jeremy sad at last, setting down his camera and grinning at her. "I bet you're about ready to drop."

Diana nodded, sinking down on the log. "That's hard work," she gasped. "I had no idea it would be like that."

"These are going to be great," Jeremy assured her.

She started to say something, but before she had a chance, he was sitting beside her, reaching out to smooth back a tendril of hair that the wind had blown across her cheek. Though he'd done that a dozen times while he was taking photographs, this time his touch was different. His fingertips caressed her cheek lightly, then came slowly down to touch her lips.

Diana's mouth felt dry and she couldn't catch her breath. "You are so beautiful, Diana," Jeremy whispered, his fingers moving to the back of her neck, "and you don't even know it."

He was going to kiss her. She knew it in that brief second and even before his lips moved closer, her eyes closed. She wanted him to kiss her, she wanted it more than she'd ever wanted anything in her whole life.

It seemed to go on forever, his lips tender and sweet and wonderful. The whole world vanished from around them, leaving just the two of them and this moment. She felt his arms around her and lifted her own hands to touch the soft hair on the back of his neck.

The magic didn't end with the kiss. When he lifted his lips from hers and smiled into her eyes, her heart leaped with joy. Nothing but love could make her feel this way, she thought — tingly and nervous, happy and frightened all at once.

"I've wanted to do that for so long," he whispered.

"Well, I'm glad you finally did," she responded. She wanted to say more, but he was kissing her again and nothing else mattered. Finally everything was right with the world. They had just parted when the sounds of approaching hoofbeats intruded and forced them both back to the real world.

Irene reined in. "Jeremy, your mother is waiting for you down at the stable. She said something about a phone call you're supposed to be home for."

"Fiona," Jeremy gasped. "She's calling tonight. I forgot all about it." He looked at his watch and groaned, then ran for his bike. "See you tomorrow, Diana," he called over his shoulder.

Diana just sat there, reveling in the wonderful feeling of being in love. And Jeremy felt the same way she did! She was sure of it now. She looked up at Irene, slightly embarrassed. "Fiona is his sister," she murmured. "She's in England."

Irene nodded. "Ready to go back?" she asked.

Diana looked around the enchanted area of the pond, noticing for the first time that the shadows were growing long and it had to be late. "I guess so," she said, all the questions and problems that she'd come here to think about flooding back into her mind. As the wonder of his kisses faded, she realized she was still confused. She knew she loved Jeremy, but now what was she going to do about John?

Chapter
11

Friday morning Diana could hardly wait to get to school to see Jeremy. Unfortunately, John, not Jeremy, was waiting for her in her homeroom when she arrived.

"How come you went riding without me yesterday?" he asked. "Irene came over for dinner last night and she said you went out all alone."

"I just felt like it," Diana replied, wondering if Irene had told him about Jeremy, too. But John's expression was as caring as ever, so she was certain Irene hadn't said a word. She shuddered to think how John would have responded if he'd even guessed what had happened yesterday at the pond. Her whole body felt warm as she remembered Jeremy's kisses, and she felt the color rising in her cheeks.

"We'll go again tomorrow," John was saying. "I don't like the idea of you riding out there alone, Diana. What if something happened to you?"

The thought amused her and she laughed. "I've been riding alone since I was five, John," she reminded him.

"Have you decided where you want to go tonight?" he asked, obviously not amused by her words. "Dancing or a movie?"

"Dancing, I guess," Diana murmured, suddenly aware that someone was behind her. The first bell rang.

"I gotta go," John said, bending to brush her lips lightly with his. "See you at six-thirty."

Diana turned around and found herself looking into Jeremy's angry eyes. She started to explain, knowing he had gotten the wrong idea about John kissing her, but he turned his back and headed for his desk before she could say a word. All the magic of the previous afternoon faded like a puff of smoke. Why did everything have to be so complicated?

Lunch on the quad with the crowd offered no opportunities for Diana to talk privately with Jeremy, no time for her to explain that she was going out with John tonight to tell him that she didn't feel the same way about him as he did about her.

Gloria was in one of her super-efficient moods, taking notes, and consulting with Woody and Peter, but mostly she seemed concerned with keeping herself as close to Jeremy as possible. Diana wondered if she was trying to make Bart jealous. A few minutes of watching objectively made her doubt it. Gloria didn't seem to care at all when Bart joked with Sasha or Brenda. She didn't even notice when girls from other groups came by to flirt or talk with him. She had obviously lost interest in Bart and now was after Jeremy, Diana thought. And he didn't look too uninterested. Suddenly she realized they were all discussing Bart's part in the video.

"What part?" Diana asked.

"I guess you weren't with us when Sasha came up with a script for the video," Janie explained. "It's to be a sort of play about how girls like us, seniors, are torn between the fun of high school and the promise of the more sophisticated world beyond."

"What a great idea," Diana said. "But how do we do it? I thought this was a silent video."

"It is," Sasha replied. "But it's up to Woody and Jeremy to find ways to show what the models are thinking and feeling without using words."

"We will have a soundtrack," Peter said. "And I'll try to pick songs that portray the emotions in Sasha's script."

"Oh, don't we sound professional," Phoebe teased. "I wonder if there are awards for junior genius in a video tape."

"We won't even get credit, let alone an award, if we don't decide where to film this epic," Jeremy said with annoyance.

"Why not the school theater?" Diana asked. "I thought that was the original idea."

"Half the class is shooting there," Woody said, looking less enthusiastic than usual. "In fact, every place we've talked about has at least one group planning to shoot there. We want to be original."

Diana looked down at her half-eaten sandwich

and sighed. What had started out as so much fun was now just becoming a lot of trouble. It seemed to be getting on everyone's nerves, including hers. She didn't know how much longer she could bear to hang around this crowd and watch Gloria hang all over Jeremy.

"Are you all right, Diana?" Bart asked, making her jump.

"I have a little headache," she said, looking at him and thinking she was glad he was her brother. He might be the playboy of the school right now, but she could see the concern in his eyes.

"I have some aspirin in my locker," he said. "Come on."

He helped her to her feet. When they were inside the nearly deserted school, he turned to her and asked, "What's going on, Diana? You looked like a punctured balloon out there."

For a moment tears threatened to overflow, but then she regained control and almost laughed at his image of her.

"You say the sweetest things sometimes," she told him.

"So what's wrong? Marquette giving you a hard time or something?"

"We're going out tonight and I'm going to tell him that I don't want to go with him. I like him as a friend, but. . . ." She couldn't go on. She really did feel lousy. She didn't want to tell Bart about Jeremy now that it appeared their time together hadn't meant a thing to him — nothing more than a few stray kisses in a romantic setting after he'd taken pictures of her. He probably had done the same thing many times before, with many different girls.

"Somebody else?" Bart asked, not abandoning the conversation the way she'd expected. He was frowning. "Be careful how you tell Marquette, Sis. I know he's been nice to you, but I keep hearing stories about stuff he's pulled in the past, and he does have a temper."

Diana felt a twinge of resentment at his words. She didn't need protection anymore. She was only a year younger than Bart, not a baby who couldn't handle her own social life.

"Just a word to the wise," Bart said. "Well, I gotta get back to lunch."

"You mean your harem," she teased. "How do you keep them all straight?"

"I just call them 'sweetheart'. It seems to work." He winked and left her to return to the sunny quad.

By Friday evening, Diana was still not sure what she was going to say to John. He arrived with a box of candy, a bouquet of flowers, and a delicate gold bracelet. His sweetness and his compliments merely seemed to compound her guilt. How could she possibly hurt him? He was so good to her.

They ate dinner at a seafood restaurant. Every time Diana made an effort to start a serious conversation, John would tell her a hilarious story about something that happened at football practice. She laughed the whole time and never had a chance to get a word in edgewise. After dinner they went directly to the Space Ship, a new dance club in Washington.

Diana was almost blinded when they walked in. Metallic banners and bizarre-looking space creatures that rose and fell at unpredictable intervals hung from all over the ceiling. The centerpiece was a flashing spaceship, its light pulsing in rhythm with the rocking beat of the music that filled the room.

There were lots of familiar faces out on the dance floor, but Diana didn't try to join any of them. Now that she was here with John, she was just going to relax and have a good time. The Space Ship just wasn't the kind of place in which to have a serious discussion.

They danced for what seemed like hours and Diana was sorry when she had to ask John to take her home.

"Come on, things are just getting started," he protested. "It's too early to go home."

"You heard my mom," Diana reminded him. "One o'clock is my curfew."

"Not when you're out with me." He looked at her with narrow eyes. "Curfews are for when you go out with little boys like Stone. You're my girl, Diana, and I want you with me for a while longer." He pulled her close.

Diana tensed. "John, that's not funny. My mother will be waiting up for me and she'll worry if I'm not home by one."

"Call her and tell her we're going to be late," he ordered. "They probably have a space phone here somewhere. You could even call her if she was on Mars." He laughed uproariously at his own joke.

"I want to go home," Diana repeated, meaning it now. She looked around for Bart and spotted him dancing with Brenda. "If you won't take me, maybe Bart will."

John glared at her stubbornly for a moment, then shrugged. "I just thought we were having a good time," he muttered as he paid the bill. "It's not like you've spent any time with me all week. I miss you, Diana. I want to be with you."

Diana sighed with annoyance. "I was having a good time, John," she began as he started the car, "but if I get home late, I'll be grounded. I won't be able to go anywhere but school if that happens."

"You wouldn't be able to go riding with me tomorrow," John said. The realization put an end to their argument, and John drove Diana home without another word of protest.

Still, she was very glad when he turned into the driveway and she was safely home.

He walked her to the door, and his gentle goodnight kiss filled her with guilt as she tried to ease away from him. She could have talked to him about their relationship, she realized, but she'd made excuses because she was afraid of his anger. The longer she waited, the harder it was going to be.

She felt relieved when she finally slipped inside and fled to her room. She had to tell him the next day, she decided. It would be easier in the privacy of the countryside, while they rode. Somehow she

111

would have to make him understand.

Irene welcomed them warmly at the stable Saturday afternoon, but Diana was constantly reminded of Jeremy as she looked around. John was in the same mood today that he'd been in the night before — bossy, possessive, following her every step. His arm was always around her, and she couldn't even talk to Irene about Galaxy and her foal without John nuzzling her neck.

"What movie do you want to see tonight?" he asked as they reined the horses through the gate and started across the meadow.

"I'm going to have to stay home tonight," Diana said. "I have an English paper due on Monday and it's going to take me the rest of the weekend to get it done."

"But I never see you," John growled. "That's no way to treat your boyfriend, Diana. We're supposed to have fun together."

"We have to talk about that, John," Diana said, gritting her teeth and preparing herself to face his hurt. "I'm not your girl friend. I like you and I've enjoyed going out with you, but. . . ."

"You want to date him, don't you?" John reined his horse so close to her mount that his knee pressed closely against hers. His face was frightening in its fury.

"What are you talking about?" Diana asked, though she had a strong suspicion she knew.

"You want to be with that camera nut, don't you? I've seen him looking at you like a lovesick puppy. Well, you can just forget it. You're my girl and he's not for you."

"I am not your girl friend," Diana stated, her temper flaring to match his. "I can date anyone I choose, and if you continue to act like this, I won't see you again."

"You can't do that! You can't go out with him tonight."

"I am staying home and working on my English paper tonight," Diana shouted back, trying not to let him see her fear.

His dark eyes blazed at her for a few seconds, then slowly the anger faded. "Can I call you tonight?" he asked.

She shrugged. "If you want to, but I won't be able to talk too long. I have a lot of work to do."

"What about tomorrow? Can you go out tomorrow?"

"I have to work on my paper," Diana repeated.

"We could drive to a country inn and have dinner," he continued. "Wouldn't you like that, Diana?"

"I have to stay home and work," Diana said again, controlling her temper with effort.

"No!" John glared at her, then spurred his mount ahead of hers, galloping along the ridge and into the trees. Diana held her horse in for a moment, then let him go, too. She needed the feel of the wind on her face and the plunging excitement of the run — it helped her burn off the anger that John had brought out. She was finally beginning to understand why both Janie and Sasha had warned her to be careful.

By the time they drove back to Rose Hill, John's dark mood seemed to have faded. He wasn't happy when she insisted on going straight home instead of stopping at the sub shop, but she escaped with one final kiss and no more scenes.

Luckily, no one was home and she had plenty of time to calm down before dinner. She immersed herself in her paper, emerging only to eat and talk to John on the phone.

She stayed home on Sunday, too, refusing to go to the sub shop with Bart, even though she knew Jeremy would be there. She wasn't ready to see him yet. She didn't know what she was going to say, how she was going to make him remember Thursday afternoon at the pond.

The weekend seemed endless and she was actually glad when Monday came. She would see Jeremy in homeroom and at lunch, and maybe she'd have the chance to tell him that things were really over with John.

Chapter
12

"She wasn't with him, John," Gloria said to John Marquette. "I spent yesterday afternoon with Jeremy and he told me he was going to spend the evening developing pictures."

"He could have gone to see her." John's face was grim. "She's my girl, Gloria, and I'm not going to let that English creep ruin things. If he goes near her, I'll take care of him."

"I live across the street from the Einersons," Gloria reminded him. "I would have seen Jeremy if he'd come over."

"Well, he better keep away from her. All she needs is a little time, then she'll realize that we belong together. It's just this dumb video thing that has her all confused."

Gloria nodded. "Jeremy thinks she should be the star of the whole show. It's no wonder he's turning her head."

"I've got to stop him," John said, striding up

and down the school hall radiating angry energy. "I've got to do something, Gloria, and I have to do it soon."

Gloria frowned at his broad back. Though she always claimed friendship with John Marquette, she sometimes felt it was like being friends with a very large and vicious dog. She worried that he would lose control of his anger and really hurt someone.

"Could I make a suggestion, John?" she said as he turned back in her direction.

"What?" He didn't sound very interested.

"Let me take care of things," Gloria said, a plan already forming in her mind.

"What can you do?" he demanded.

"If Jeremy is busy with me, he can't be busy with Diana, can he?" she asked, flashing him a teasing smile.

"He won't be so attractive to her if I pound his face in," John growled.

"Do you really think Diana would forgive you if you did that?" Gloria asked. "She'd just feel sorry for him, John. She might even like him more if you hurt him because of her."

John swore and paced away from her again. "What if she doesn't come back to me?" he asked.

"Maybe you should get her a ring," Gloria suggested. "Tell her how much you love her and ask her to wear it. Yes, that's it, a friendship ring."

John glared at her for a moment, then slowly his expression changed. "You really think it would work?" he asked. "You really think she'll

116

go out with me if I give her a ring?"

"How could she resist?" Gloria asked. "She's a lucky girl to have someone like you to care about her."

He grinned widely and lifted her into the air. "I'll do it!" he shouted, then set her on her feet again and disappeared down the hall.

Gloria leaned back against her locker, her knees weak with relief. That should do it, she told herself. Now all she'd have to do was make sure that Jeremy knew all the gory details of John's courtship. She got her books out of her locker and hummed to herself as she walked to her homeroom.

"Good morning," Diana called to Jeremy when she got to her homeroom, smiling at him. "Did you get your English paper done?"

"Finally," he said. "How about you?"

"Spent most of the weekend on it," Diana replied. "I just hope I did okay. I want to get off to a good start in my classes here."

"Is that why you weren't at the sub shop yesterday?" Jeremy asked.

"I. . . ." Diana started to explain, then stopped abruptly when she noticed John standing in the doorway. He brushed past Jeremy as though he wasn't there.

"Just came by to tell you that I'll have a surprise for you next weekend," John said. "Something special for my special lady." He touched her cheek, then turned to fix Jeremy with a glare. "*My* special lady," he repeated as he left the room.

Jeremy started to say something, but before he could get out a word, Diana turned and ran out after the big wrestler. Jeremy sighed and sank down at his desk. So it was all true, everything Gloria had told him. Diana really was going with Marquette, and those kisses Jeremy and Diana had shared hadn't meant anything. He didn't even look around to see if she'd come back by the time the bell rang.

Nothing went quite right for Diana after that. She couldn't catch up with John in the hall and when she returned to her homeroom, Jeremy didn't even look in her direction. There was no way she could approach him or explain — especially since she had no idea what John had been talking about. But she had to talk to John to tell him to leave her alone.

It was the same at noon. Jeremy was friendly, but distant. He turned to Gloria for comments and ideas. He really seemed to be avoiding Diana, yet he continued to insist that she was going to play an important part in the video. She couldn't make sense out of his actions.

Things went on like that between them all week. Finally, unable to bear it any longer, Diana cornered Janie after school on Thursday. "Can I ask you a question, Janie?" she asked.

"Of course," Janie said with a gentle smile.

"Why does Jeremy want me in the video?"

"Because he thinks you'll be wonderful," Janie said. "He told us how terrific your pictures came out and he's sure that you'll be even better in action on video tape."

"He has the pictures he took of me?" Diana was stunned at the idea.

Janie nodded. "I guess so. He was talking to Henry about them the other day. Didn't he show them to you?"

Diana shook her head. "He's hardly talked to me since he took them. I thought maybe they were so awful he didn't want me to see them."

"Why don't you go over to his house and ask?" Janie suggested. "You have a right to see them."

"I couldn't do that," Diana protested.

"Why not?"

"I couldn't just drop in on him," Diana murmured nervously.

Janie's eyes were full of understanding. "I know it isn't easy, Diana," she said, "but if you really care about him, you should go over and talk to him. Nothing's going to change if you don't confront him."

Diana took a deep breath and smiled. "Thanks, Janie," she said. "Maybe I will go see him."

Diana headed for the bike rack and unlocked her bike. Janie's suggestion was starting to sound like a good idea. She'd been past the handsome house the Stones owned several times, so she knew where Jeremy lived. She pedaled off in that direction, her brow furrowed as she went over various conversations in her head.

She still hadn't decided just what she was going to say by the time she reached his house, but the hurt inside her was too deep for her to turn back. Squaring her shoulders, she went up to the front door and rang the bell.

"Diana!" Jeremy looked surprised.

"Hi," she said shyly.

They stared at each other for a few awkward seconds, before Jeremy stepped back and opened the door wider. "Come in," he said, obviously flustered.

Diana looked around curiously, admiring the handsome antique chest that stood to one side of the foyer and the finely crafted Oriental screen in the other. Then she realized that Jeremy was standing in the doorway staring at her. "Janie said you'd developed the pictures of me," she murmured.

"I was going to make you a set of prints," Jeremy said, "but I couldn't decide which ones to enlarge for you."

"Could I see them?" Diana asked, feeling awkward standing in the entry.

"Yeah, sure. Follow me. My studio's in the basement." Jeremy led her down the stairway to the basement. "My parents let me convert the playroom into a studio and darkroom so I finally have a place where I can work," he explained, switching on the lights.

Diana froze at the foot of the stairs. Her own face looked back at her from all sides of the studio. Dozens of enlarged photographs were mounted on boards and hanging on the walls, photographs that literally took her breath away.

They were her and yet they weren't, for she'd never seen herself look like the girl in the pictures. She was confident, proud, and beautiful. The camera had captured delicate shadows, glowing highlights, laughter, and excitement.

"I can't believe they're me," Diana gasped, looking from one to the other. "How did you do it?"

"I just photographed what was there," Jeremy replied. "I didn't do anything. I had an idea of what they'd look like, that's why I was so anxious to take your picture, so you could see how the camera would capture you."

Memories of the afternoon at the pond flooded her mind as she looked closely at each picture and remembered the moment it was taken. Then she stopped in front of a picture that wasn't taken at the pond. "When did you take this one?" she asked.

"Phoebe's party," Jeremy answered. "Some of the others are from around school."

"I didn't even know."

"I hope you don't mind. I just couldn't resist." He looked miserable. "If you want one for your boyfriend. . . ."

"I don't have a boyfriend," Diana answered, her heart pounding so hard she was sure he could hear it across the room.

"What about Marquette?"

"I told him last Saturday that I didn't want to go out with him exclusively. I thought we could still be friends, but now I'm not so sure. He keeps following me around and referring to me as his girl." She spoke quickly, anxious to get the words out before she lost her nerve.

"But Gloria told me he was getting a ring for you," Jeremy said. "She said that you two were an official couple."

"I never told her that," Diana cried out. All of

a sudden a horrible suspicion began to form in her mind. "Maybe that's what John meant when he said he had something special for me next weekend." She wondered how much Gloria had to do with it.

"You didn't know what he meant?"

"Of course not," Diana assured him. "I'm never going to date him again. He's scary when he gets angry, Jeremy. And he acts like I'm his property and I'm not, especially not after what happened last Thursday afternoon." The words were out before she thought and she could feel herself blushing.

"You mean that?" Jeremy asked. Then before she knew what was happening, he was beside her, his arms around her, holding her so tightly she could barely breathe. But it felt wonderful and she clasped her own arms around his back to press him even closer. "Oh, Diana, I was so afraid that you really cared for John," he said breathlessly, between kisses.

She laughed with pure joy when he finally let her go. "And I thought that you and Gloria were getting involved," she confided. "I was even thinking of dropping out of the video because I couldn't bear seeing you with her."

"We're just friends," Jeremy said. "She's been pretty helpful with the video, that's all. I think she's kind of lonely.

"But let's not talk about her," Jeremy said. "Let's talk about what we're going to do."

"What's that?" Diana asked, allowing herself to be led to a battered old couch against the wall.

"This," he said, kissing her eyes, her nose, her

cheeks, and finally her lips. The final kiss lingered until her head was whirling with the thrill of it. They both laughed with surprise when they broke apart. What a relief it was to finally have told him how she felt. She thought she was going to burst with joy as she sat there snuggled in the crook of his arm, his free hand lazily caressing the back of her neck and now and then running through her hair.

"So, do you want to go to the football game with me tomorrow night?" Jeremy asked.

"Of course I do," Diana replied.

"And the dance afterward?"

"That, too," she said, lifting her face toward his for a final kiss before she left. It was soft and sweet and she lost herself in it. This was the way it was supposed to be, she just knew it.

Chapter
13

"Do you believe this assignment?" Phoebe asked. "How can anyone be cruel enough to give a quiz the day of the first football game?"

"History teachers don't live in the same time period as normal people," Chris replied. "Haven't you noticed how Ms. Halloway's eyes light up when she talks about knights and jousts and all that stuff? Mention football and she just looks blank."

"She does make history come alive, though," Sasha added. "When she describes the way things were back then, I can just picture myself living in a castle in medieval France."

"So I remember," Phoebe groaned. "You were the one who said it was such a romantic period of history that we'd all love to spend an extra week on it."

"It was a romantic time," Janie said, "but the

124

tests are definitely of the twentieth century."

"And that's when we could fail them, too," Brenda agreed. The girls were all gathered in the basement family room at the Halls' house to study together.

"At least it will be over before the football game," Chris said. "You are all going, aren't you?"

Sasha nodded. "Bart offered me a ride to the dance."

Brenda looked surprised, then she laughed. "Me, too," she admitted, "and I wonder who else he'll be taking. Harem transport must be his specialty."

"Well there's safety in numbers," Phoebe said. "So at least Bart will be safe."

"What do you think of him, Brenda?" Sasha asked.

"That no one should take him too seriously," Brenda warned. "He likes to flirt too much."

"I think it's because he was hurt so badly leaving Maryann," Sasha commented, her expression full of sympathy. "You know how painful it can be when you have to leave someone you really care about."

"Who's Maryann?" Phoebe asked.

"The girl in Montana," Sasha replied. "Didn't he tell you about her? They were real serious about each other, but they decided to date other people now that they're so far apart. That way they'll see if their love is real enough to endure."

"He spent an hour telling me a similar story," Brenda said, "but I could swear the girl's name was Trudy."

"You're right," Janie agreed. "He told me, too, at the Space Ship one night. He was real upset. He said Annie was dating his best friend now."

Sasha put her history book aside. "Isn't that interesting?" she said.

The girls looked at each other for a moment, then broke out in hysterical laughter. "No wonder he keeps a harem here," Brenda said. "He must have had one there, too. Let's see, we have a Trudy, a Maryann, and an Annie."

"And heaven knows how many others," Sasha said. "He's spending time with half the junior girls and some of the underclassmen, too. He must have invented a different name for every girl."

"I wonder," Janie said, shaking her head in amazement. "Do you really think there is a girl he left behind?"

"Probably a whole school full," Chris said.

"And not a single one he was serious about," Brenda agreed. "I think he'd remember her name, if there was one."

"The fink," Sasha groaned. "I really felt sorry for him with that sad story. What a dirty trick."

"And how careless of him," Chris commented. "I mean, if he's going to tell everyone a story like that, he should at least try to remember what he said."

"So what are we going to do about it?" Brenda asked, her eyes sparkling with mischief. "I mean, he's a menace to female hearts, so we should make him pay, don't you think?"

"Tomorrow night," Janie agreed. "I think the dance would be the ideal time." They quickly formulated a plan and then returned to studying.

On Friday Diana felt like she was floating on a cloud. She barely noticed when John glared at her from across the hall, or when Gloria frowned at her when she sat down beside Jeremy at lunch. She couldn't remember ever feeling so happy.

Gloria, on the other hand, was miserable. It was impossible to miss the bond that had suddenly formed between Diana and Jeremy or the sparks they gave off when they were together. Jeremy had announced that he was taking Diana to the football game and the dance afterward, so Gloria knew her plan had backfired. She went in search of John Marquette.

"What's going on?" John demanded before Gloria even said a word. "I saw Stone hanging all over Diana earlier today and I don't like it."

Gloria shrugged, a little frightened by his tone of voice. "He's taking her to the game and the dance tonight."

"I thought you were going to keep him busy," John growled.

"I tried, John. I couldn't be with him every minute."

"Well, he's not taking her to that dance, I can tell you that," John said. "I've got the ring and I'm going to give it to her after the game. She'll just have to tell him to get lost."

"Maybe you should just wait a few days," she began, envisioning a terrible scene at the dance. "I mean it's just one dance and. . . ."

"She's my girl," John snarled, "and he's not

taking her anywhere." As he strode away, Gloria had the sinking feeling trouble lay ahead.

Diana pulled on her red pants and slipped a red-and-gold-patterned sweater over her head. She brushed her hair out and let it fall around her shoulders in soft waves, smiling in anticipation of the evening ahead of her with Jeremy.

Jeremy, Monica, and Peter arrived fifteen minutes early to pick her up. She felt like she was floating when Jeremy greeted her with a gentle kiss. "Henry and Janie promised to save us good seats," he said, taking her hand.

"I can hardly wait," Diana said. "My first Kennedy High football game." They held hands the whole way to the game, and again Diana glowed with the overwhelming sense of happiness.

When they reached their seats, and greeted Henry and Janie, Jeremy looked around with an intensity that made Diana curious. "What is it?" she asked.

"This is fantastic," he replied.

"It's just a football field," Henry said. "One hundred yards of grass surrounded by wooden bleachers. What's so great about that?"

"Football is so American, and it's an important part of high school, right?" Jeremy's eyes were glowing with excitement. Henry nodded while everyone else stared at Jeremy. Then, suddenly, Diana understood what he was getting at. "The video!" she shouted.

"This place would be the perfect background

for the evening gowns," Jeremy said at last, his eyes focusing on Diana. "I can just see it.

"We could do it early in the morning," Jeremy continued, "when the sun comes streaming through the bleachers. That is east, isn't it?" He pointed.

"I've been here early and it is pretty great-looking," Woody said. "You're a genius, Stone. Let's get together tomorrow and do some planning."

Just then, the teams came running out onto the field. The crowd roared its enthusiasm. Diana had no trouble picking out the players that she knew — Ted, Bart, and of course, John. She waved to Bart, then looked away as John waved back. She wished that Henry had saved them seats higher in the bleachers so they wouldn't be so close to the Cardinals' bench.

The band, which was seated in the section next to them, began to play, ending all conversation and thought of anything but the game. It was glorious. The Cardinals played well and Bart seemed to contribute a good deal, catching several of Ted's passes without difficulty. By the half, they were ahead by seven points.

The only dark cloud on Diana's horizon was John. Even the two rows of people that separated his bench from hers didn't prevent her from feeling his animosity every time he looked her way.

The second half of the game was even more exciting. The score was tied until the very end, and all the fans were on their feet as the final play began. The other team had the ball when a

Cardinal player suddenly intercepted a pass and raced back up the field and into the end zone for the winning touchdown.

"We won! We won!" Diana shrieked, her throat already raw from cheering.

Jeremy threw his arms around her and his lips found hers in a celebration kiss. Diana was aware of nothing but his body pressing into hers. When his embrace finally relaxed, her heart was racing. Embarrassment swept over her as she realized she'd forgotten that they were surrounded by a crowd.

"Who made the interception?" she gasped.

"Your boyfriend," Gloria snapped.

Diana looked out to the field and saw that everyone was pounding John on the back, but the big player didn't look happy. His gaze was directed her way and his face was twisted with fury. She stood frozen in horror as John headed toward them.

He didn't stop at the team bench. He pushed his way into the first row of spectators, shoving them aside as he came after her. He reached out and grabbed her arm as she tried to scramble away from him.

"What do you think you're doing, Diana?" he demanded. "You're my girl and you have no business kissing this wimp."

For a moment she was afraid to speak up, then her anger erupted. "I am not your girl, John. I never was. You have no right to tell me what to do or who I can be with."

"You're mine!" John turned from her and

lunged at Jeremy. "You leave her alone. She doesn't belong in your lousy film, and I don't ever want you touching her again."

"Diana isn't your property and she can do anything she wants," Jeremy began, then ducked as John swung a huge fist in his direction. Jeremy stumbled back into the crowd, nearly falling through the bleachers as everyone scrambled out of Marquette's way.

Diana screamed as Ted, Bart, and several other football players came after John, grabbing his arms and dragging him back down the bleachers to the bench. "Get out of here, Diana," Bart shouted over his shoulder as John tried to struggle out of the other players' hold.

Jeremy grabbed Diana around the waist and dragged her away from their seats. Since the crowd was dispersing, they had no trouble losing themselves in the crush. Still, they didn't stop until they reached the refuge of Peter's car.

"Are you all right, Diana?" Jeremy asked, his strong arms tightening around her. "He didn't hurt you, did he?"

"No, I'm fine. What about you?" Diana reached out a trembling hand to smooth back his hair. "Did he hit you?"

"I ducked." Jeremy began to laugh.

For a moment she felt sick, then the absurdity of it swept over her and she began to laugh, too. "I'm sorry," she said.

"It's not your fault," Jeremy assured her. "Some people just aren't good losers. I don't blame him for wanting to keep you. I would want to hit anyone who tried to take you away from me."

"No one ever could, Jeremy," Diana whispered just as his lips silenced their laughter and led them back into a magical world.

Chapter
14

The music was already blaring when they got to the gym. Diana paused in the doorway, scanning the crowd. "Don't worry," Jeremy said, slipping an arm around her shoulders. "He's not going to bother you again."

"If you're worried about Marquette, don't be," Henry said. "I heard someone say that the coach would probably cut him up into little pieces once he got him to the locker room."

"If he shows up here, the whole school will attack him," Monica said. "He's not exactly popular."

Diana sighed. "That's too bad," she said. "He did make the winning touchdown. He should be celebrating it."

As Diana, Janie, and Monica headed to the restroom, Janie let them know a surprise was in store for later in the evening.

"What are you talking about?" Diana asked.

Janie smiled. "That's all I can say. I've been sworn to secrecy."

"Oh, that's cruel!" Diana cried.

"All I can tell you is to try to be near Bart at ten-thirty sharp."

"Bart?" Diana frowned at her. "What's going on?"

"She won't tell us," Monica warned, "so we might as well go and do some dancing before ten-thirty."

Though she longed to know more, Diana had no chance to ask Janie any other questions. Jeremy claimed her as soon as they returned to the main room, and Henry and Peter whisked the other girls away. Once they started dancing, Diana forgot about the mystery and just enjoyed herself.

She only saw Bart once all evening when he came over to talk to her and Jeremy.

"How are you two doing?" he asked. "Everything cool?"

"Super," Diana answered, smiling up at him. "How about you? You were terrific in the game."

"Merely great," Bart replied. "I'll save terrific for next week when we'll need it more."

"What's that mean?" Diana asked, sensing that he wasn't teasing.

"Marquette's benched for the next game, maybe two. The coach was really mad at him."

"I hope everyone doesn't think it's my fault," Diana said, feeling guilty. "I told him last weekend I didn't want to go out with him exclusively. I don't know why he went so crazy tonight."

"Don't worry about it, Diana. Nobody's blaming you. Everyone knows what he's really like," Bart said. "The team was amazed that he managed to be so nice for so long. World record for him, I guess."

"I just hope he learned his lesson," Jeremy said. "And knows enough not to try something like that again."

"He was pretty well cooled off by the time the coach got through yelling at him," Bart said. "I think he knows pursuing Diana is a lost cause." He grinned. "Well, I'd better get back to the dance floor. I've got a lot of girls to keep happy."

Jeremy shook his head as Bart walked away. "I don't know how he does it," he said. "If anybody else came in with six girls everyone would hate him — including the girls."

Diana giggled. "That's Bart," she said. "He's always been like that, but he does seem to be getting worse since we moved here."

"I don't see how he can be happy," Jeremy whispered, as he took her in his arms to dance. "How can dozens of girls be better than one special girl?"

That didn't seem to require an answer, so Diana just rested her cheek against his shoulder and closed her eyes. Nothing could be better than this, she was sure.

Bart was a little surprised when Janie came across the dance floor and stopped in front of him. "I believe this is our dance, Bart," she said, her brown eyes sparkling with excitement.

Bart looked at Brenda. "Go ahead, Bart," she

said. "We can dance the next one."

Bart shrugged, then grinned at Janie. "Where's Henry?" he asked.

"He wanted to talk to Peter for a minute," Janie said.

"Special request?" Bart guessed.

"Something like that," she said, but she didn't meet his inquiring gaze.

The moment they reached the middle of the dance floor, the music came to a sudden halt and the lights came up. Peter spoke into the mike. "I've just been handed a special announcement," he said. "It seems that someone here is getting an award. Bart Einerson, this is for you."

Bart stiffened, then glanced down at Janie. She looked like she was about to explode with laughter. "What's going on?" he demanded.

Janie reached into the pocket of her jeans and produced what looked like a gigantic bandage, made out of construction paper. She pinned it solemnly to his chest. "From Annie for your broken heart," she said, then stepped back.

"From who?" Bart began, but before he could go on, Sasha was approaching with an identical patch.

"From Maryann," she said.

"From Trudy," Brenda said, attaching her bandage.

All three girls surrounded him and at that moment the lights dimmed and the music began again. "Want to dance?" they all said at once. Bart had a sheepish expression on his face as he shook his head no.

He was grateful for the dim lights when he felt

his face burning with embarrassment. Then suddenly the ridiculousness of the whole thing swept over him and he had to laugh. "You really caught me," he said.

"Let's just say you have enough bandages to keep your broken heart together for the rest of the year," Brenda said.

Gloria crossed the room to where Diana and Jeremy were standing. "What in the world was that all about?" she asked.

Diana laughed. "I think Bart's tall tales caught up with him at last. He never was very good about keeping his stories straight." She shared a smile with Jeremy as he led her back out on the dance floor.

On Saturday, everyone involved in the video project met on the football field to discuss Sasha's revised script. They blocked out moves and practiced poses until they were ready to drop.

By the time they finally adjourned to the sub shop, Diana's legs ached from climbing up and down the bleachers and her head throbbed from trying to remember the constant commands from Woody and Jeremy. She settled in the backseat of Woody's car with a sigh, wondering if everyone else was as tired as she was.

"Kim was the smart one," she groaned. "I didn't know it would be such hard work."

Phoebe giggled. "Being a star is tough, huh? I guess I'm glad I just have a bit part."

"Kim wanted to be in the video," Woody protested, "but she's so busy with the catering business, she wouldn't have had the time to rehearse."

"It's going to be worth it," Jeremy said, pulling Diana close to his side. "Just wait till you see it on tape. No other group is half as inventive. Maybe we'll even get to show it at a school assembly."

"You guys get all the glory and we do all the work," Phoebe teased. "We're not even getting credit for it."

"We're just the unsung heroes," Sasha sighed. "My first screenplay and no one will know."

"Of course they'll know," Woody protested. "Our video will have credits just like any television show. You'll be listed as the writer, Sasha, and everyone else will be cast or crew."

"Maybe they'll hand out Cardies," Phoebe murmured.

"What?" Jeremy asked.

"Little Cardinal statues, like Emmys or the Oscars." Phoebe looked perfectly serious, except that her eyes were dancing with fun.

"When are we going to do the real thing, Jeremy?" Diana said.

"I was thinking about next Saturday morning," he answered. "How's that for everyone?"

"Do you think we'll be ready by then?" Woody asked. "We have until the middle of November to turn the tapes in."

"We only have the dresses until the end of October," Phoebe reminded him, "and if we get them dirty or anything, we need to give Henry time to get them cleaned or fixed."

"I think we should do it now while the weather is still good," Jeremy said.

"Okay, let's make it Saturday," Woody said.

"Then, if we have to tape it a second time, we'll have Sunday morning to try again."

"How can you think we'd be anything but perfect the first time?" Diana joked.

"Because I watched the rehearsal," Woody growled, pulling into the sub shop parking lot. "Which reminds me, we're going to have to do something about Gloria."

"What do you mean?" Diana asked.

"She moves like a robot," Woody replied. "She's trying hard, but she's much too self-conscious."

"You don't think she'll get over it?" Sasha asked.

"We have to turn the tape in this year," Woody answered. "What do you think, Jeremy?"

"She looks great in the dress, but every time she moves, she draws attention away from everybody else with her stiffness." He sighed. "We can't cut her out of the video, though."

There was a moment of silence. Then Diana leaned forward. "What if you had her sitting down the whole time instead of moving?" Diana suggested.

"That would make an interesting visual contrast," Jeremy said, giving her shoulders a squeeze. "It's nice to have a girl with both beauty and brains." With that they all climbed out of the car and filed into the sub shop.

Chapter
15

Diana spent the rest of her free time on the weekend with Jeremy. They went to a movie on Saturday night and on Sunday he came to dinner at her house. Her parents were entranced with him and impressed with how much work had gone into the video, as Diana and Jeremy described what was involved in the planning. When they heard his taping was to be done early the following Saturday morning, her mother insisted that the entire group come to breakfast when they were done.

Diana barely had time to enjoy her newfound relationship with Jeremy once the school week started. Not only were there fittings for the dresses and two rehearsals at the football field, but she had a math quiz and a history paper due, too.

On top of all that, she noticed that John was still keeping close track of her. She saw him hiding in the back of the theater, stalking around the football field while they rehearsed, lurking around outside of her homeroom. He said nothing, did nothing, but he was always there.

The only other sour note in her week came on Thursday from Gloria. She wasn't happy with her smaller part and she made a point of letting everybody know. She complained constantly, disrupting the rehearsal and making everyone unhappy. She even objected to the football field location and predicted dire problems with their early morning schedule. Then as they finished their final rehearsal Thursday afternoon, she announced that she'd heard that two other groups were planning to use the football field for their video. With that she turned and left, leaving the rest of them to solve the problem.

"That's too bad," Diana murmured. They'd been careful to keep their plans secret from the rest of the video class in the hope that no one else would think of using the field. "Does anyone know what their themes are?"

"One is about football," Jeremy said, "so that won't be like ours, anyway. I have no idea what the other one's about. Let's just hope they don't plan to tape at sunrise on Saturday," Jeremy continued, "and that the weather holds."

"And that the models don't fall over their feet," Diana added.

"You'll be sensational," Jeremy told her. "This future Oscar-winning filmmaker knows how to recognize talent. Trust me."

"Zat's right, Diana," Woody said, in an exaggerated German accent. "Trust him, little girl, he vill make you a star." He twirled an invisible mustache and wiggled his eyebrows at her.

"I trust you two," Diana assured them, giggling. "It's my ability to keep from falling on my head that worries me."

"Don't think about it," Jeremy advised as they got on their bikes and started pedaling toward her house. "Just think about going to the game with me tomorrow night and what great company I'll be."

He gave her a quick hug good-bye in front of her house, then left her to do her studying. Diana put her bike in the garage. As she started for the door, a voice behind her made her jump.

"Aren't you two just too cozy for words?" John snarled, stepping out from behind a big old tree at the side of the house.

Diana gasped and took a step back. "What are you doing here, John?" she demanded. "Spying on me?"

"Watching you make a joke of yourself over Stone." His tone was contemptuous. "He's going to make a fool of you in that tape. It's a bunch of nonsense the way I hear it. But maybe I can stop it before it's too late. You're my girl, Diana, and I plan to have you back. You're going to wear my ring and no wimp with a camera is going to stop me."

"No way!" Diana stated. "You might as well give up, John. You made a fool of yourself last time, so don't do it again. I wouldn't go out with you if you were the last boy on earth, so why don't you just quit following me and spying on me? Go bother someone else." She opened the door with a hand that barely shook, stepped inside, then collapsed against the door in relief.

Why couldn't he leave her alone? She tried not to think of what he might do to spoil the video. She just hoped that he'd stay away from Jeremy and her at the football game, and he wouldn't crash the party Woody was having at his house afterward.

Diana was on the lookout for John all day Friday, but he was nowhere to be seen. Perhaps the angry exchange outside her house had been enough for him. He didn't even look her way at the football game, just sat on the bench and watched in grim frustration as the Cardinals struggled without him. It was a tough game and Diana was ecstatic when they managed to win by one point when their opponents' try for the extra point went astray.

After the game, she rode to Woody's party with Jeremy, Janie, and Henry. Once there, she spent time talking to Sasha about the interview series Sasha was writing for the school paper, agreed to help Chris with a student government project, and promised Phoebe that she'd be on the decorating committee for the school's Halloween dance.

She finally felt at home with the whole crowd now and she seemed to be forming a special friendship with Janie. Diana found she could talk to her about anything. She even told her about John's threats — something she hadn't confided to Jeremy since she didn't want him to have anything else to worry about the day before the taping.

Janie sighed and shook her head. "You're

143

braver than I am. I can never talk back to him. Maybe he'll leave us alone now, anyway. I mean, what can he do, really? He's not going to make trouble with Bart and Ted and so many of the other football players in the cast with us. He's in enough trouble with the team for last weekend."

"I guess you're right," Diana murmured. "I'll just be glad when tomorrow is over."

"Me, too," Janie said. "I love wearing anything that Henry makes, but I'm not sure I want to see myself on the screen. The thought of it makes me kind of nervous."

"Don't even talk about being scared," Diana said. "I get butterflies every time I look at my dress."

"But you were super in rehearsal," Janie said. "I could see everything Sasha wrote in your expressions. It was like you were living it."

"I was," Diana said. "That's the only way I could do it. If I think of being in front of the camera, I freeze."

"Just do it the same way tomorrow and we'll all be famous soon," Janie teased.

"I'll settle for just being finished with the video," Diana replied.

The sky was barely rosy Saturday morning when Diana and Bart left the house. Diana shivered in spite of the big wool cape she wore, but she had a feeling her shivers were more from nervousness than the morning chill. They arrived at the football field to find chaos.

Bart, Ted, and one of the other team members were in their football uniforms, while the

144

rest of the yawning boys, including Peter Lacey and Dick Westergard, were in dark suits and white shirts. They were complaining about the hour and teasing the girls about being all dressed up with no place to go. Diana hurried over to kiss Jeremy hello, then joined the rest of the girls and waited for the taping to begin.

Jeremy was everywhere at once, getting people into position, checking the equipment, clearing litter from the bleachers. Excitement and enthusiasm radiated from him like electricity. The cold and the darkness vanished, and Diana felt herself slipping into the mood of the scene. She took her opening position on the bleachers on Woody's signal.

The sun edged slowly over the rolling hills and spilled dramatically through the bleachers in barred shadows. Diana shivered as she waited for Jeremy's cue, then when it came, she moved. She was the girl caught between her longing to stay with the football hero of her high school dreams, and the need to go up to the beckoning college boy above her on the rising bleachers.

She moved with Janie and Chris, changing places, drawn first to one love, then to the other. Brenda and Phoebe entered and made their choices, while Diana alone stayed seated between the two poles of life. The final shot focused on her anguished longing and confusion.

"And that's it!" Jeremy shouted.

"We are super," Woody crowed. "We don't have to do it again. It was like a movie scene. I could almost hear the music Peter is going to play with it. You were all terrific."

"We really did it, didn't we?" Diana shouted. "It went so fast I can't believe it."

"And after so much rehearsal," Phoebe agreed. "You'd think it would take longer."

"If you want to go through it again," Woody suggested, then ducked as everyone turned on him. "Just kidding," he protested. "You were all much too good to have to repeat it. What do you think, Jeremy?"

"I think we should start practicing our acceptance speeches for those Cardies that Phoebe suggested they award," Jeremy said. "It looked flawless to me."

"We finished just in time, too," Janie said. "Look who's here."

Diana turned and felt a chill on her spine as she recognized John Marquette's bulky form. "What is he doing here?" she asked.

"I don't think we should wait to find out," Jeremy said. "Let's just take our equipment and get out of here."

"Amen to that," Bart said. "I want to get out of this football uniform and go eat. Mom was cooking up a storm before we left. I'm starving."

Laughing merrily, they gathered up their props and equipment and headed for the waiting cars. The video was taped, now it was time to celebrate.

Chapter
16

Woody, Jeremy, and Peter spent Sunday afternoon editing the video, so Diana joined Janie and Henry at their workshop, helping to fix up the evening gowns. They'd all been very careful, but there were two hems that needed to be redone and one dress with splinters that had to be removed. It took a while before they had them all pressed and back in their bags ready for delivery to the store.

Diana wandered around the cluttered workshop looking at Henry's designs. "These are really terrific, Henry. I can understand why all the stores want your clothes. You're so talented. When I've saved up some money, I'd like to place an order."

"I'd love to design something for you," Henry said with a slow, gentle smile. "You'd look good

147

in almost anything. I could try something really unusual."

"You mean it?" Diana asked, intrigued.

Henry's eyes suddenly lit up. "Would you model something for me, Diana?"

"Now?"

He nodded. "Do you have time?"

"To try on one of your designs? Sure," Diana said, looking at him with the wide-eyed excitement of a child in a toy store. "What do you want me to wear?"

"This." Henry lifted a garment bag from the back of a rack. "It should be all right with your black stockings."

"Not Diana, Henry," Janie protested. "That's more the sort of thing Laurie wears."

"Just try it," Henry urged, grinning now. "I think you'll be surprised."

"Okay," Diana said, heading for the other room to change clothes.

The outfit was a shock: a cropped, red leather top and a miniskirt of textured black leather, cut higher on one side than the other.

Diana put it on, grateful for the black body suit she'd worn that day, since the top exposed her midriff. It really needed cowboy boots and a more exotic hairstyle, she decided, but the effect was startling when she had a chance to view herself in the full-length mirror.

"This is wild, Henry," she gasped.

"You look fantastic," Janie said. She looked at Henry. "You were right again."

"Who is this for?" Diana asked, entranced with

her reflection in the mirror. "I mean, is it for someone at school?"

"It's for a boutique in Washington. They asked me for a half-dozen samples to show their customers. I have one more to do."

"Could I see the others?" Diana asked.

"Sure. These are the drawings," Henry said. "You can try on any of the others if you want to. Janie's modeled this one." He pointed to a sketch of a long, full-skirted calico dress. "I haven't seen the rest on anyone."

"Which one do you want to try on next?" Janie asked.

Before Diana could answer, the phone rang and Henry called to her to talk to Jeremy.

"Sorry to interrupt you, Diana," he said, "but I really wanted to talk to you." His voice sounded concerned.

"What's wrong, Jeremy?" she asked, her mind flooding with suspicions about John. "What's happened?"

"It's the tape."

"Do we have to do it over?"

"No, it's great," he answered, "better than we thought it would be. It looks almost professional." He should have been excited, but he wasn't.

"So what's wrong?" Diana demanded.

"It's only three-and-a-half minutes long, and we need a five-minute video for the class."

"Can't you make it longer? Did you edit out too much?"

"We've worked on it all afternoon, Diana, and everything we've tried has spoiled the effect. It's perfect the way it is, but it's a minute-and-a-half short." He was obviously very disappointed and at a loss for how to solve the problem.

"Just a second," she said, turning to tell Janie and Henry the news. "We'll be right over to talk about it," she said, getting back on the phone.

"Thanks," he said. "Can't wait to see you."

The line went dead before she could say anything more.

Jeremy's studio was brightly lit, but the faces that greeted them were grim. Even Woody, ever the optimist, looked depressed. "Here we are, true geniuses, stuck with a useless video," he said.

"It's not useless," Diana said. "If it's as good as you say, everyone should see it."

"But we can't turn in a short video," Jeremy reminded her. "We wouldn't get credit for it. The assignment is for a five-minute tape."

"Can't we add to it?" Henry asked. "I mean, shoot more scenes to go with it. We haven't sent the dresses to the store yet."

"It would ruin it," Woody said. "We talked about it, but it would definitely look lousy if we tacked more on the end."

As Diana looked at the sad faces, an idea struck her. "Hey, what about making this a two-parter?" she suggested. "I mean, this is a fashion video, right? So who says we can't have a second segment with totally different clothes and a new setting?"

"Are you serious?" Woody asked.

Diana looked at Henry to see if he caught on. She was relieved when he nodded.

"It would certainly be a contrast," Janie said, "but I don't know. What kind of a background could we use?"

"The outfit I tried on gave me an idea," Diana continued. "What about Danberry Stable? Horses, green grass, trees, the stream — a natural background and those funky clothes. What do you think?"

"What funky clothes?" Woody asked.

"The stable?" Jeremy mused.

"It sounds like the only answer," Peter said. "A second segment could give us the length we need."

"We'll have to work in something to tie the two together," Woody said.

"We can decide on that after we see how the segment comes out," Jeremy said. "What do the fashions look like?"

"Come on over to my workshop and I'll show you," Henry said. "I only have five of them done, but I'm working on a sixth."

"I think we'd better call Sasha," Woody said. "We might need another script."

"We'll have to talk to Irene Danberry, too," Diana reminded him. "I don't think she'll mind having us tape there, but I haven't talked to her since John and I. . . ." She let the words trail off.

"Want to go there now and ask her in person?" Jeremy asked. "We could meet the rest of you later at the sub shop. Unless you want me to see the clothes first?" He looked from Woody to Henry to Peter.

"Mind if I go too? We can take my car,"

Woody said. "I think we can trust Peter and Monica's judgment on the clothes."

Jeremy nodded. "And Diana's already seen them. So, why don't the three of us go to the stable?"

The gloom lifted from the group. "I'll bring the sketches to the sub shop," Henry suggested. "Then everyone can see them."

"Use the phone to call everybody," Jeremy called over his shoulder, "and we'll see you at the sub shop."

He paused in the hall to give Diana a grateful hug, then they followed Woody out to his car. "I just hope this works out," Jeremy said. "I wonder how we can tie the two segments together."

Diana shrugged. "Maybe Sasha will have an idea," she said. "It sort of depends on how you want to do the segment, doesn't it? I mean what kind of story we have."

Jeremy chuckled. "You're learning," he said.

"She'll probably end up making films and starring in them," Woody said, grinning at them both. "You've created a competitor, my man, and I think she's going to be great. You going to join our class next semester, Diana?"

"I think I have my hands full without that, thank you. I just happened to be trying on one of Henry's new outfits when you called and you sounded so miserable, I had to think of something."

Jeremy kissed her lightly. "I'm glad you did," he said. "Now just keep your fingers crossed that nothing goes wrong."

"This gate is great," Woody said as they turned in at the stable, "and those buildings should be a good background for bright clothes."

"I was thinking maybe we could shoot in the paddock or meadow," Diana said, her mind racing. "And maybe Bart and some of the others could ride horses behind the models. What do you think?"

"Sounds good to me," Jeremy said. "What do you think, Woody?"

"I think it'll work," Woody said. "Now who do we talk to?"

Within minutes, Diana found Irene in the stable and brought her out to talk to Jeremy and Woody. Irene leaned against the stable wall and listened, fascinated, as the two boys explained the video to her. It was obvious that she was pleased at the idea and soon they were shaking hands on the deal.

"So you'll be shooting Saturday morning," Irene said.

"Weather permitting."

"And you'll let me know how many horses you'll need by the middle of the week?"

"We will," Woody said. "And we'll pay rental on the horses, too. I'm just sorry we don't have a budget to pay for using the location."

"Don't worry about that," Irene assured him. "I can hardly wait to watch you work."

Jeremy started to speak when a loud voice interrupted him. "What's going on here?" They all turned to face John Marquette as he emerged from the stable door.

"They were just telling me about a video they're making for a class at school," Irene said. "They're going to shoot a segment here, John. Isn't that exciting?"

"How could you?" he roared, glaring first at his sister, then at Diana. "You'd use anyone, wouldn't you?" he snarled, taking a step toward Diana. "You and your sneaky little boyfriend are going to be sorry. You're not going to use this place for your stupid video!"

"Now, listen John, I don't know what's going on, but I can tell you . . ." Irene began, but he didn't wait to hear her. He headed for his car and was speeding down the narrow road before any of them could say a word.

Irene turned to Diana. "What's the matter with him?" she asked. "I thought you two were friends."

Haltingly, Diana tried to explain. She could feel the red flaming in her cheeks and tears burning in her eyes. "If you want to change your mind about giving us permission to tape here, we'll understand," she finished. "I wouldn't want to cause any family trouble."

"John's temper is *his* problem," Irene said. "I'm sorry that you aren't still going out because I think you were good for him, but I don't want to stop our friendship. You and your friends are more than welcome to do your video here and I hope you'll still come out and ride whenever you want."

Diana was touched by the sincerity of the offer and she had to swallow hard before she could thank Irene. Jeremy and Woody added their voices to hers and in a moment the ugliness was past and Diana could think of what lay ahead and not about John's threats. By the time they reached the sub shop, they were full of ideas for the video and anxious to talk them over with the rest of the crowd.

Chapter 17

The meeting at the sub shop went on forever as they all pitched in with new ideas. Sasha finally put everything together and came up with an outline for another script.

"The two sequences will represent two entire different aspects of life," she explained. "The conventional sequence that we already did and the rebellious side in the new segment. The clothes fit the images of girls doing their own thing but at the same time they attract the eye of the old-fashioned cowboys. How does that sound to everyone?"

"You've sold me," Peter agreed.

"Do you think we can be ready by next Saturday?" Woody asked. "I mean, we had more rehearsal time for the last part."

"We're experienced now," Phoebe told him. "And we have all week to get ready."

"We can do it," Jeremy said.

"Sure we can," Diana agreed, trying not to think about the look on John's face when he'd said they'd never shoot at the stable. "When do we start rehearsals?"

"First you'll need a script," Sasha reminded her. "And I still have some homework to do tonight. I have a free period tomorrow, though, and I'll do my best to have something for you after school, okay?"

"We couldn't do it without you," they all shouted at once, confidence running high now that they had a plan.

Sasha presented them with the script the following day, then refused a part in the segment, saying, "I've got to spend the week working on *The Red and the Gold*. I've been neglecting it since you got me involved in the video and I really can't let it go any longer. Call me if you need any changes."

To keep it short, they decided to use only the five outfits that Henry had completed after Monday's fitting session. Chris, Brenda, and Phoebe joined Janie and Diana as models. It was only then that Diana remembered Gloria.

"Did anyone call Gloria to tell her about the new video?" she asked, looking around at everyone gathered in Henry's workroom.

"Why?" Chris asked, her expression cool. "We don't need any more models."

"Well, no, but. . . ." Diana felt a little guilty. "She did work on the first section."

"So did Laurie," Phoebe reminded her, "but we only have a minute and a half, so not everyone can be in this part."

"She was pretty unhappy about her part in the last one, anyway," Janie murmured. "And there isn't anything for her to do in this one, so why make her miserable?".

Diana reluctantly agreed that they were right and decided not to tell Gloria.

But somehow she found out about it. She showed up in the school theater for their rehearsal at noon. But she didn't complain about not having a part and she didn't offer many comments on the new segment, so after a while, they hardly noticed that she was there.

Gloria saved her complaints for John Marquette, calling him each night to tell him exactly what was happening with the group's new video. He listened and said little, which made her wonder what he had in mind and why he was still interested in what Diana was doing. Finally, on Thursday, she got up the nerve to ask. "Why do you care about the video, John? You don't still want Diana for a girl friend, do you?"

"No, but they have no right using the stable," John said. "That was our special place — the first place I ever took Diana. We saved the foal together. She has no right to take everybody else there."

"Well, your sister gave them permission to shoot Saturday morning, so they're going to," Gloria said. "She doesn't seem to care whether you're dating Diana or not."

"She should." The phone clicked dead in her ear.

Diana was exhausted by Saturday morning.

They'd done everything they could in rehearsal, but there was still a great deal that would have to be decided on at the stable. She sat up in bed and looked out her window, then heaved a sigh of relief. At least the weather was still cooperating. It was another glorious fall day.

Since this wasn't a single sequence shot, they were starting early. Diana dressed in the outfit right after breakfast, substituting red tights for the black ones she'd worn the first time and adding her own black cowboy boots. She left her hair loose since Laurie had joined them Thursday and volunteered to do everyone's hair and makeup for the segment.

Diana was feeling a little apprehensive when she and Bart drove the station wagon over to pick up Jeremy and the equipment, but that faded the moment she saw Jeremy's face. He was so excited he almost glowed and his kiss dissolved all her worries. What could go wrong? she asked herself. It was going to be just as terrific as the first video.

Irene welcomed them warmly to the stable. "I've got everything ready," she said. "The only thing I have to ask is that you stay away from the back pasture. Eddie Hogan, the used car dealer, has brought in a truckload of wild horses. He's going to have some kind of promotional auction to open his new lot in Georgetown and he's asked us to board them until then."

"Wild horses?" Bart grinned. "How wild?"

"You can't get close to them," Irene said. "They're going to have to be worked for at least a couple of weeks before he can even auction them.

Personally, I think he should be shot for doing it, but the horses would probably have ended up being slaughtered if he hadn't and this way they may get decent homes."

"If you want some help training them, give me a call," Bart said. "Both Diana and I have worked with wild horses, so we could try our hands at gentling them."

"You've got a job," Irene said. "You can take a look at them after you finish filming today."

"You got it," Bart promised. "Now I'd better get to work."

Everything went smoothly as they did the shots with Chris and Phoebe near the gates and the stable buildings. As she waited for her turn, Diana could feel the excitement rising. They moved to the small front pasture and Laurie finished Diana's hair and turned her attention to Brenda.

"I think we'll just use Janie, Diana, and Brenda for this one," Jeremy said as he, Peter, and Woody set up the equipment on a small rise about halfway between the fences that separated it from the stableyard and the back pasture. "Janie and Brenda will move from the opposite side of the pasture toward Diana. She'll be in the middle holding a horse — black, if possible. Bart can ride in the background and Ted, maybe you could lean on the fence near the stable, waiting for Janie to come over for the final shot. Okay?" He looked to Woody.

"Sounds right to me," Woody agreed.

"How about the black gelding John rode the first time you came out?" Irene asked Diana. "I can have him saddled in a minute."

"Let's just put a show bridle on him," Diana suggested. "He's a beauty, so he'll look great without tack."

They walked through the entire sequence once, then again, trying variations, getting the feel of the moves, laughing and talking. Then it was time to tape it. Diana led the big black gelding away from the others, calming him as he snorted his excitement.

There was a flash of movement near the fence and Diana was surprised to see Gloria walking along the back fence line. She'd arrived later than the others and said little, but now it appeared that she wanted to be in this video, after all. Diana tossed her hair out of her eyes, and decided not to point out Gloria's presence to the others.

"So are we ready?" Woody shouted.

Diana nodded and off to her left Brenda waved the big Stetson hat that Woody had borrowed from the school prop room. Janie moved forward, wearing the calico dress.

The action began and the taping went even more smoothly than their final run through had. They went through the entire sequence without a break. Then just as Bart exited through the gate and Janie started to move toward Ted, Diana heard a sound behind her. She turned, expecting to see Gloria, but she was nowhere in sight.

Diana's scream caught in her throat as a herd of horses came over the rise in the rear pasture and headed directly toward the gate between the two pastures. It was now standing wide open!

The wild horses were charging straight at them. "Get out!" she shouted. "Everybody out of the pasture!"

The gelding leaped nervously when she yelled and she nearly lost the reins, but instinct tightened her grip as he dragged her a few steps. "Steady, fella," she soothed, lifting the knotted reins over the horse's head and gathering them with a lock of mane to help her vault onto his back.

The horse leaped forward the moment she was settled, nearly unseating her since she had no saddle. She gripped hard with her knees and turned toward the horses. They were already streaming through the gate, wild-eyed with terror. She looked around and saw Brenda running for the fence, then heard her scream as she tripped and fell. She was too far away for Diana to reach her before the horses did.

The herd was headed directly toward the small rise where Woody, Peter, and Jeremy were standing surrounded by their equipment. Diana took a deep breath and dug her heels into the gelding's sides, riding right into the leaders of the herd. She dropped the reins on the gelding's neck, using her knees to guide him as she began to shout and wave both hands in the air.

For a moment, she wasn't sure it was going to work. Then the lead horse faltered, slowed, and turned aside, bumping another horse and throwing it off stride. Within seconds, the whole herd was slowing, milling, kicking. The stampede was over. Diana stopped shouting and looked over her shoulder.

Irene was riding in with Ted following her, and Bart was on his way to the fence with Brenda riding behind him on his horse. He'd obviously managed to scoop her up before the terrified horses reached her.

"Let's herd them back into the other pasture," Irene called.

Diana, Ted, and Bart hurried to help her and in a few minutes the wild horses were moving back through the gate and the danger was over. "Who opened the gate?" Bart asked. "It was shut during rehearsals."

"Gloria was wandering around back here," Diana said, "but she wouldn't have let the horses in. She's scared of them."

"You kids go back and make sure everyone is safe," Irene said, riding through the gate, then closing it. "I'll find out what happened." She followed the straggling herd of horses over the rise and out of sight.

"Is Brenda all right?" Diana asked as they rode back.

"You should have seen Bart," Ted said. "He did it just like on TV. Scooped her right up off the ground."

"Years of practice," Bart said. "Diana and I used to win the rescue race every year."

"Everybody okay?" Diana asked as she reined in the dancing black gelding in front of the group now gathered by the fence.

"Thanks to you," Woody said. "That was some trick riding."

"I wish you'd tell us when you plan these surprise endings," Jeremy said, his grin not quite hiding the concern in his eyes. He held out his arms to catch her as she slid off the horse. "I almost didn't get it all on tape."

"You taped it?" Diana gasped, remembering the video for the first time.

"I think I got it all," Jeremy replied. "Unless Woody dragged me away too soon."

"I was afraid he'd get a closeup of horses' hooves," Woody said, "but you turned them in time."

"The hat seems to be the only casualty," Brenda said.

"I wonder what happened to Gloria," Diana said, looking around.

"She left before you started shooting in the pasture," Laurie volunteered. "Afraid she might have to help, I guess."

"She's still around," Bart said, standing in his stirrups. "Her car is over by Laurie's. And guess whose car is parked up by the house?"

Diana followed his pointing finger and swallowed hard as she recognized John's car. "You don't think . . ." she began, then saw that everyone was looking across the pasture. "Oh, no." She felt sick as she saw the riders approaching. John was with his sister and Gloria was walking along on the other side, looking terrified.

"I found him in the pasture with this," Irene said, holding out an opened soda can, shaking it slightly so they could hear the pebbles rattle inside.

"You scared the horses, John," Diana gasped. "How could you? Someone could have been seriously hurt."

"It was just a joke. I wanted to jazz up your little movie." His sneer didn't cover the angry shame on his face. "I told you, you had no right to bring them here, Diana," he snarled. "This was our place."

There was nothing she could say to that, so Diana turned her attention to the girl beside him. "And you helped him," she said. "Why, Gloria?"

"He said he'd teach you a lesson," Gloria sobbed. "I didn't know about the horses. I didn't want anyone to be hurt. I just wanted you to know that you can't snub people all the time. I have feelings, too." Her sobs rose to a crescendo and she turned and fled. Chris went after her to try to get the whole story. Everyone else looked back at John. He sat there silently, embarrassed, then reined his horse around.

"I don't know what to say," John began. "If any of your equipment was damaged, I will definitely repay you. I don't know what got into me. Seeing Jeremy and Diana together just made me go nuts, I guess. But I never meant to ruin your film. . . . I'm sorry, I really am."

"We may not need to reshoot a thing," Jeremy said. "In fact, if I got a usable tape of the stampede, we'll probably have the most exciting video of all."

"Not exactly what was in the script, but it could be great," Woody agreed.

"How soon will you know?" Irene asked.

"As soon as we get back to my place to work on it," Jeremy said.

"And you're sure you're all okay?" Irene asked.

The assurances came with laughter and relief

as they finally realized that they had, in fact, survived the excitement. Then there was nothing to do but pack up the equipment and return the horses to their stalls. Diana spent an extra moment with the black gelding, before she followed Jeremy and Bart to the station wagon.

"What happens now?" she asked.

"We all go to my house," Jeremy said, "and the rest of you can fix some lunch while Woody, Peter, and I see what we have. How does that sound? My mother promised to stock the refrigerator with all sorts of goodies for us before she and my father left for the day."

"Fine with me," Bart said. "Just as long as it involves food. Rescues make me hungry."

When lunch was made and the girls carried the trays down to Jeremy's studio, the three boys emerged from the back looking grim. "What's wrong?" Diana asked.

"We have a real problem," Jeremy said.

"Oh, no," Phoebe wailed. "Did you forget to put in the tape?"

"Pheeberooni, that's cruel," Woody said. "The problem is we have two of the best tapes you ever saw."

"Two?" Diana asked, her heart lifting as she saw the glow in Jeremy's eyes. "What do you mean?"

"Thanks to the stampede, we have over five minutes in the stable sequence," Jeremy said. "We won't be combining them. We'll just use the football segment as an extra-credit assignment." He came over and put his arms around Diana, pulling her close.

"I can't believe it's over," she said, feeling a touch of sadness at the thought. "It was so exciting and now. . . ."

"What do you mean, over?" Jeremy asked, his lips close to her ear. "We're a team now, Diana, we'll be doing all sorts of things together."

He loosened his embrace enough so that he could look down into her eyes. The noisy crowd around them faded into the background. As his lips found hers, she knew that he was right. The real excitement was just beginning — it came from being together and being in love.

COUPLES

Coming Soon. . .
Couples #15
COMING ON STRONG

When Ms. Tyler came in, the class grew quiet. She quickly took the roll, then looked around the group. "We have a new student joining us today," she announced. "A junior named Holly Daniels. She's transferring in from Mr. Hoover's section."

Bart watched her, then realized he was staring at her. She was so pretty it almost took his breath away. Holly Daniels. Her name fit her perfectly — she looked pure and fresh.

He couldn't believe he had never seen her before. How could he have been in the same building with her for the past six weeks without noticing her? But then, it was a big school, and the people he knew were either part of his crowd, in his classes, or on the football team. The other girls he knew were ones who let him know they were there — like Heather and Kristi Marshall — the ones who obviously wanted something from him. This girl, he could tell immediately, wasn't anything like that.

168

"We're going to continue our discussion of government financing today," Ms. Tyler continued, breaking into Bart's thoughts. "We were talking about U.S. Treasury Bonds. What is the face value of a government bond?" She looked around the circle. "Bart?"

He nervously cleared his throat, his pulse racing. "It's always a thousand dollars." he said carefully, his voice strained, "but the market value can be more or less. It depends on whether current interest rates are lower or higher than the day the bond was issued."

"Excellent, Bart," Ms. Tyler nodded. "You've done your homework. Now, can someone else tell me how often the fixed return on the bonds is paid and how bonds can be purchased?"

Bart knew that Holly had looked at him when he had answered the question. He felt just like he did when a big football play was coming up — excited, ready to meet the challenge, but scared to death that with a false move he could ruin everything.